# After Dinner Conversation Themes
## *Government Ethics Edition*
*Philosophy | Ethics Short Story Fiction*

# After Dinner Conversation *Themes* – Government Ethics

This magazine publishes fictional stories that explore ethical and philosophical questions in an informal manner. The purpose of these stories is to generate thoughtful discussion in an open and easily accessible manner.

Names, characters, businesses, organizations, places, events, and incidents are either the product of the author's imagination or are used fictitiously. Any resemblance to actual persons, living or dead, events, or locales is entirely coincidental. The magazine is published monthly in print and electronic format.

All rights reserved. After Dinner Conversation Magazine is published by After Dinner Conversation, Inc., a 501(c)(3) nonprofit in the United States of America. No part of this magazine may be used or reproduced in any manner without written permission from the publisher. Abstracts and brief quotations may be used without permission for citations, critical articles, or reviews. Contact the publisher at **info@afterdinnerconversation.com**.

ISBN# 979-8-9896194-7-4

Copyright © 2024 After Dinner Conversation
Editor in Chief: *Kolby Granville*
Edition Editor: *Kolby Granville*
Story Editor: *R.K.H. Ndong*
Copy Editor: *Kate Bocassi*
Cover Design: *Shawn Winchester*
Design, layout, and discussion questions by After Dinner Conversation.

*https://www.afterdinnerconversation.com*

***After Dinner Conversation*** *believes humanity is improved by ethics and morals grounded in philosophical truth and that philosophical truth is discovered through intentional reflection and respectful debate. In order to facilitate that process, we have created a growing series of short stories across genres, a monthly magazine, and two podcasts. These accessible examples of abstract ethical and philosophical ideas are intended to draw out deeper discussions with friends, family, and students.*

# Table Of Contents

FROM THE EDITION EDITOR ............................................................................... - 4 -

THE BOOK OF APPROVED WORDS ..................................................................... - 5 -

THE DRAFT ............................................................................................................ - 14 -

FOR YOUR SAFETY ............................................................................................... - 31 -

UNDERSTANDING ICE CREAM ........................................................................... - 39 -

PROHIBITION ....................................................................................................... - 55 -

THE DECAY ........................................................................................................... - 71 -

THE KILL REGISTRY ............................................................................................ - 88 -

THE CRATE ........................................................................................................... - 103 -

FORM SEVEN ALPHA ........................................................................................... - 124 -

EUTHANASIA ........................................................................................................ - 149 -

AUTHOR INFORMATION .................................................................................... - 160 -

ADDITIONAL INFORMATION ............................................................................. - 163 -

\* \* \*

# From the Edition Editor

The purpose of this book is to review the role of government in promoting and discouraging behavior by limiting our liberties through rules or taxes. Government is, by its very nature, in the liberty limiting business, which when you de-politicize the concept, should be fine to most. Show me a place without a liberty limiting government, and I'll show you a place you don't want to drink the tap water or drive a car.

Of course, the real debate is when, and for what reasons, government should act, or refuse to act, to regulate the interactions of people and/or businesses. This is a difficult discussion because most people blindly rush to tell you what their media/family/tribe have told them to tell you.

Getting people to *think*, therefore, requires stories that use a bit of sleight of hand. You can't ask people if they support gun control by the government, instead, you have to write a story about another world with "all weapon control" covering slingshots to suitcase nukes. You have to search the absurd!

Those are the stories I have picked for this edition; stories that come at issues from a side angle so as not to trigger our internal scripts that take the place of thought. Enjoy! I also want to dedicate this book to Hugh Hallman, Neil Giuliano, Dennis Cahill, and George Washington Plunkett, who collectively taught me everything I know about politics and government.

Kolby Granville – Editor

# The Book of Approved Words

*W.M. Pienton*

* * *

I relaxed on the couch watching an illegal show on videotape. "They had such freedom of language back then," I thought.

"I told you to *sit*, retard," the man on the screen shouted.

Reluctantly plopping down, the other man mumbled, "Faggot."

"We can't get away with those words anymore," I thought, turning the volume down. When the episode finished, I shut off the VCR and TV. "Back to work," I mumbled.

I am an Approved Writer and have to regularly update my published works, deleting words recently made illegal. Sitting, I read from my laptop: "The pink, blue, and white sky reminded me of Easter." Earlier this year the word "Easter" was made illegal. It excludes non-Christians and is now considered offensive.

\*\*\*

Two hours later, I leaned back in my chair rubbing my eyes, thinking, "Can't take anymore today. I really should be using the latest edition of the *Book of Approved Words*. I'd get evaluated if I missed something." A colleague was recently imprisoned for using an illegal word. There were even rumors he was executed. I do not know if he was rebelling, or simply using an out-of-date book.

Not wanting to end up like him, I left the house and took a bus to the Bureau of Acceptable Language.

\*\*\*

Approaching the desk, I asked for the latest edition of the book. "You'll need to turn in your old copy," said the bespectacled woman.

"Why? I never had to do it before."

"It's a new law. Once turned in, the old copies will be destroyed so all traces of the offensive words will be swept away."

"I noticed the price's gone up."

"Leader needs to fund his reeducation programs. Upon returning with your old copy you'll be fingerprinted."

"That's new too."

"It's to keep track of writers and help find word criminals. Oh, and don't forget to renew your writing license."

Nodding, I left the building.

\*\*\*

Returning home, I flopped onto the couch and paged through my outdated book. "I don't want it destroyed." I gazed at my bookshelves, thinking, "Well, I still have my copies from previous years." Snapping the book shut, I returned to the bureau.

I placed the book on her desk and she handed me a clipboard of forms. Filling them out, I returned it. "Alright sir, come this way for fingerprinting."

* * *

Taking my new book, I thanked her and left. It gets thinner every year. If it continues like this we will be left with *no* words.

* * *

I entered the house finding my brother on the couch. "Hey Pete," he said, standing. I quickly shut the door and drew the shades.

Silas *was* an Approved Writer. Last year he knowingly published an article using illegal words then went into hiding. Word Crimes even summoned me for questioning. I worry for him daily.

"You alright? What are you doing here?"

"I'm fine, but the Freedom of Speech Movement needs your help," he said.

Originally labeled a hate group by the government, they were recently recategorized as terrorists. The Freedom of Speech Movement wants no word off limits, no subject taboo. They formed a little after the Bureau of Acceptable Language.

"I dunno. Maybe."

"You have a rebellious streak, just not as pronounced as mine. You know Thomas Jefferson said, 'I hold it that a little rebellion now and then is a good thing, and as necessary in the political world as storms in the physical.' It's sad most people don't know who he was anymore."

Tossing my jacket onto the couch, I sat. "I'll think about

it. Tell me what you need."

"I need to scan the old books dad and grandpa left you."

"What happened?"

"The bureau found and destroyed almost everything. We need to build a new database."

"What if the bureau discovers where the scans came from?"

"Nobody but *me* will know, not even other members."

Silas always kept his word. I sighed, "Why not. Coffee?"

"Sure," he replied, sitting. He looked about the room and said, "Videotapes, huh?"

"The black market doesn't exactly have a plethora of mediums to choose from."

"Oo you said 'plethora.' That's illegal you know," he teased.

"Shut up," I smirked. "I have deadlines to meet. If I miss one they'll check on me so you'll have to scan them yourself."

"That's fine. The equipment's in my bag."

"It's gonna take at least a week," I said, sitting and handing him a mug. "After our coffee I have to write."

"To success," he said, clinking his cup to mine.

*  *  *

We worked all night. After finishing the article I helped scan. Morning found us relaxing on the couch. We each had a tumbler of whiskey.

"Remember Melody?" slurred Silas.

"Yeah, I had a crush on her. She wrote poetry so I wrote some hoping to impress her."

"That's why you started writing."

"What about her? How's she doing?" I asked, taking a sip.

"She's gone Pete, evaluated."

We sat in gloomy silence. "Damn." Glancing at the clock, I said, "I need some sleep. I have to appear before the Bureau of Acceptable Language board today."

"What for?"

"Someone complained about a movie review I wrote, again."

"Oh boy."

"You got the couch. I'm going to bed."

\* \* \*

"You believe the wording is appropriate?" asked board member one, not looking up from my article.

"Yes," I replied, trying to sound confident.

"And what's the message you're attempting to convey?" asked board member five.

"I thought it was pretty clear ma'am," I said.

"Is it to make the reader happy? I'd like to hear your intention."

"What are you trying to communicate?" asked board member one.

"I didn't care for the film. It's my honest opinion," I said.

"This is the *third* negative article you've written in a row," said board member five.

"You're too pessimistic," said board member four.

"They just have to stop making bad movies," I said.

"We're taking you off movies and reassigning you to musical album reviews."

"Be positive," said four.

"But honest," added three.

"You may go," said the chairman, gesturing.

* * *

"How'd it go," asked Silas, looking up from his work.

Taking off my jacket, I said, "I've been reassigned to writing music reviews."

"So, basically a warning."

"Yeah. 'Too pessimistic,' they said. One of them told me to be positive while another said to be honest."

"What'll you do? Write sugarcoated reviews?"

"Yep. I'm going into the next room and listening to this album. You keep scanning."

"Since you *have* to be positive just write the review without listening to it," said Silas as I closed the door. "It's gonna be awful," he added, muffled on the other side. "They *all* are these days."

Turning on my stereo, I poured a whiskey preparing for the worst. The music started and I winced. I turned it off thirty seconds later and wrote a sterling review. I opened the door and Silas grinned, saying "Done already?"

"Couldn't even finish the first song. I gave the album five stars. The bureau loves it when I use stars. No words necessary."

"Good, take over for a bit. I need a break," he said, rubbing his eyes. Standing, he gave me the handheld scanner. "You know, the Freedom of Speech Movement is planning something big. I wasn't gonna tell you but we couldn't find anyone else."

"What do you need *me* for?"

"Access to the Bureau of Acceptable Language. Only Approved Writers like you can email submissions to media outlets. They blindly publish anything they're sent, too afraid of the bureau to say no. We want to submit an old dictionary."

"The board will find out."

"Yeah, *after* it's published."

"Probably won't work," I said, "And even if it does, change won't happen overnight. I'll have to go into hiding like you. Police will tear the house apart. They'd take or destroy *everything*."

"Before we publish the dictionary my friends will move your things to a safe house."

"You know the word 'dictionary' was made illegal last year. The board says that it's too intimidating and makes people feel stupid," I said, stalling.

"Where do we look up words now?"

"The Book of Approved Words has taken over the job," I said. "If I did this, I'd be leaving behind everything I worked for."

"*Everything* you write is monitored. You've never published a sentence you wanted to write and *you* live under constant threat of evaluation."

I gazed around the room remembering our dad and grandfather. Sighing, I put my head down. "I suppose it's time to move on."

"Excellent," said Silas.

* * *

The house was empty. It was early morning. We sat on the floor in front of the laptop. All that was left was to send the dictionary.

"They'll publish it," assured Silas, "if they don't wanna get evaluated. They know the penalty for questioning an Approved Writer's submission."

"I just hope the board doesn't catch it for a while," I said, sending it and turning off the laptop. We left the house. At the end of the street, I turned looking one final time upon my old life.

"Ready?" Silas asked.

"Let's go."

"It's getting light out."

"Right now the sky kinda reminds me of Easter with the pinks, blues, and whites."

\* \* \*

*This story first appeared in the After Dinner Conversation—July 2021 issue.*

## Discussion Questions

1. What are the reasons the government seems to want to remove words from the dictionary?
2. Does removing offensive *(or hate speech)* words from publication help limit the use *(or spread)* of those words *(or thoughts)* among the public?
3. What does the society think will happen if people are aware of the words they are missing? Is their action likely to get them closer to their goal?
4. Should there be forbidden knowledge or thoughts? Would you support a law that kept books that taught homemade bomb making from being printed and sold to the public?
5. Do you think there are more *(or fewer)* words being used now, than there were 200 years ago? Why is that so?

\* \* \*

# The Draft

## Jan McCleery

\* \* \*

Throngs of people entered the fifteen-story building crowned by the gold sign reading, *Center for the RTL Headquarters*. Most had no idea what *RTL* stood for.

Valets were running back and forth in front of the building, taking the next expensive car in the long line that circled the block before entering the curved driveway. Men in tuxedos and women in cocktail dresses emerged from their cars. Servers passed out champagne to those in the long line waiting to enter the building. Once inside, they entered a massive conference room with huge screens on several walls displaying the words *Center for the RTL*. A live five-piece orchestra played chamber music. Servers with trays of upscale appetizers circulated the room as the attendees milled about, greeting business associates. Empty champagne glasses were promptly replaced.

Congressman Mitch Mitchell and his wife, Gloria, were a handsome couple in their early fifties. Mitch had been swept into his seat in Congress in the 2022 midterms when he was only thirty, running on a strict pro-life platform. As they stood talking to a billionaire contributor and his wife, the lights dimmed. A deep male voice reverberated from above: "Welcome to the grand opening of the Centers for the RTL. Now… here is the founder and CEO, Dr. Celeste Rivers."

A trim woman with intelligent green eyes and short dark hair framing her pixie face eagerly took the stage and walked into the spotlight. The screens around the room projected her image. Smiling. Beaming. Charismatic. She doubted anyone knew she was thinking about how needing a hysterectomy all those years ago in college had been such an unexpected blessing, leaving her free to pursue a Stanford PhD in engineering and accomplish what had become her life's goal: to give all women in America a choice whether or not to bear a child. Now it had become a reality. Her heart beat in her chest with a combination of pride and excitement.

"Thank you all for coming," she said, her voice strong and clear. "What you will see and hear today will amaze and thrill you. It is the beginning of an era of new freedom for all women! The letters R-T-L stand for 'Right to Life.' As of today, all women can embrace the right to life without relinquishing the right to control their bodies."

The women involved with the project for the past ten years started applauding wildly. Others clapped politely but looked confused.

Celeste continued, "Today, we have the technology to allow a fetus to grow safely and healthily, from embryo to a fully developed newborn, without using a woman's body." She paused. "Behold, the incubators."

The screens displayed pictures of the center's incubation rooms. Dimly lit, each room was filled with hundreds and hundreds of incubators: some pods contained small fetuses with enlarged heads and small limbs curled into a C-shape; others held nearly full-grown babies. It was like an eerie scene from a science fiction movie.

The mood in the conference room quickly changed; some gasped. Celeste was prepared, and the screens quickly changed to a series of beautiful babies wrapped in blankets and held by their beaming mothers.

"Babies who are gestated in our incubators are healthier. No more preemies born too early due to their mother's medical issues. No more crack babies or those addicted to alcohol. Healthy babies who will bond with their mothers. Gretchen, model your baby cord for us, please."

A beautiful, tall, young, Germanic woman, all in red from her hair to her luscious lips and down to her bikini and spiky heels, mounted the stairs to join Celeste on the stage, towering over her. Low on her waist hung a gossamer silky string.

"What is that I see you wearing?" Celeste asked mischievously.

"My red bikini?" Gretchen answered her rehearsed line, spoken with a heavy German accent while flashing a smile.

Celeste winked at the audience. "She knows." People laughed, men nervously because they couldn't help staring at the striking woman on the stage.

"You mean this?" Gretchen pointed to the gossamer string. "It's my 'baby cord.' It's letting me feel what my baby is doing, just as if he was right here in my tummy." She patted her flat, bare stomach.

"Do you mind if a few of our guests feel what you do?"

"I don't mind. My husband is fascinated by it."

Celeste motioned to the audience. "Come toward the stage." She didn't need to urge. Men were pushing to get forward. Gretchen knelt, and Celeste leaned down and held a mic as the stunning woman let a few people take turns placing their hands on her stomach.

Every monitor had gone to split screen, half showing the beautiful Gretchen letting men feel her bare stomach; the other half displayed an image of her baby in the incubator, kicking and squirming.

In turn, each exclaimed, "Wow!" "I felt it kick!" "That's amazing!"

Celeste laughed. "Thank you, Gretchen."

The tall redhead stood, smiled sweetly at the men, and left the stage.

"We've placed one thousand RTL Clinics at prior Planned Parenthood sites plus added hundreds more in rural areas. Any woman can easily get to one of our clinics, where her fetus will be removed and whisked to the nearest center to be placed in an incubator. Near the end of term, the mother will be notified and given an appointment date."

On the screens, a swaddled baby is taken to a seated mother, who immediately puts her newborn to her breast to nurse. Her husband sits by her side, his arm lovingly around her. In the next view, the couple stands up with their baby, is handed a "New Baby Gift Bag," and walks out the front door.

Celeste added, "Better than the stork!"

Laughter and excitement filled the room.

"Now, are there any questions?"

A woman reporter was the first to raise her hand. When Celeste pointed to her, she pushed her horn-rimmed glasses further up her nose. "Judith Baker, *Today's Times Magazine*." She pursed her thin lips. "Are you playing God here?"

Everyone quieted. A few gasped at the implications.

"Believe me," Celeste responded, "we wrestled with difficult questions. Think of it. We could eliminate babies with gene defects. Alter survival rates based on sex, race, or other traits. Create a master race." Her voice had gotten louder as she raised her eyebrows, a look she knew made her appear sinister, and she looked around the audience. Not everyone was smiling. In fact, some looked shocked.

"But that would be playing God, wouldn't it?" Celeste chastised. "That would be altering the natural balance and plan. We said 'No!' Rest assured. We are not playing God. We are providing an alternate womb for women. Plain and simple."

Some people nodded approvingly. Celeste pointed at another reporter.

"Annie Walker, *World News*," the woman said. "What if the mother didn't want a baby?"

"Good question. After her fetus is extracted, she has up until the time of full gestation to decide whether, at the end, she wants to claim the baby or put it up for adoption. Same as the current US law. Next?"

A male reporter raised his hand. "Gerald Cross, ALT Cable News," he opened. "Won't this result in significantly more babies born per year? We all know many women buy smuggled contraceptives and abortion pills, and there are ways for women to obtain illegal abortions. Now women and their doctors will have no reason to take that risk. Won't we end up with millions of babies without mothers?"

Celeste shrugged her shoulders and didn't answer.

Gerald countered, "But what's the plan? Won't all these extra babies overwhelm the system?"

Celeste smiled sweetly. "That's an excellent question. Why don't you answer it for us? For the past few decades, the political party your station supports has pushed for every fertilized egg to result in a baby. They have outlawed contraception and all abortions. So, if there is now a problem of too many babies, it is up to your party to solve it. Next question?" And with that, she looked away from Gerald.

\* \* \*

**The Women's Revolution**

Soon, all women were taking advantage of the free service. The gossamer strings became a sign of motherhood, like a rounded, protruding belly had in years past. No longer having to deal with stretch marks and bulging stomachs, expectant mothers wore bikinis at the beach to show off their baby cords.

Released from the need to use their bodies to grow babies, women used their newfound freedom to pursue higher education, and the number of women in better-paying jobs increased. More women entered the government and formed a new political party, "The Women's Right to Life" party, and soon women were in control of the country: Congress, the White House, and most state governments.

As Gerald from ALT News had predicted, before long, the availability of babies had overwhelmed adoption agencies and the foster system.

The government created the "Office of Equality and Fairness" (OEF) to resolve the problem and established "The

Draft" system. According to Draft rules, all males between the ages of sixteen and fifty must be entered into a lottery to determine which among them would, under penalty of law, take the unclaimed babies.

Of course, men fought back, whining it wasn't fair to select only males to take unwanted babies. The OEF's answer came first in the form of questions: Who, for centuries, were forced to subject their bodies to the strain of growing unwanted babies? And who were often left to raise those children with no support from anyone, no matter how many children they already had? Who had to leave school—sometimes as young as sixteen years of age—and despair of ever being able to secure a better future? The answer: Women. "Well," the OEF argued, "now is the time for men to step up, take their turn, and accept responsibility."

The Draft Rules were solidified, and men realized the law would not be changed, not in the near future.

On January 13, 2050, "The Draft" went into effect.

\* \* \*

### January 13, 2067

Tim Mitchell woke up when four-year-old Curt jumped on him and pummeled him in the face. Tim grabbed Curt's hands and held him firmly, trying to quiet his aggression.

The sun was barely up. Having reached the age of fifty, Tim knew this was his last year; after this, he would no longer be eligible for the Draft. He had ducked it for the first sixteen years after it was established, but for the last four years in a row, he had been a big loser and was now raising four children under the age of five.

Curt, his first child, was born with a rare genetic disability that left him with cognitive learning problems as well as anger issues. He barely spoke and still had to be spoon-fed and diapered. Tim had to quit his job to raise Curt.

When Curt was diagnosed, Tim's fury was directed at his father, former Congressman Mitch Mitchell, who had been a fervent advocate to end all forms of birth control and abortion.

Tim had called his father and screamed, "What were you guys thinking? What did you imagine would happen if abortions and contraception were outlawed?" But Tim knew his father was tired of being blamed. Tim's mother still blamed Mitch for Lizzy's death. Tim's sister had committed suicide when she found herself pregnant in college. She was Congressman Mitchell's daughter, and abortion was not an option. Now Mitch's son had joined the blame game. Mitch hung up on him.

Max and Lucy, ages two and three, heard the commotion and padded into Tim's bedroom in their one-piece PJs. Tim carried screaming Curt into the kitchen. Max and Lucy followed him. Tim left Roger, less than one year old, in his crib.

The three were eating their cereal—well Max and Lucy were, Curt was throwing his—but Tim couldn't wait any longer. He turned on the TV. He'd missed the standard opening, the pomp and ceremony, but it was always the same.

*The President greets the emcee, who comes on stage with a great deal of fanfare, clapping, and music. "Elmer Greco," the President says, smiling. "Are we ready for this year's excitement?"*

*Elmer is a flamboyant man. His hair is waved up too high in front, and his white teeth gleam. He's got on too much makeup, even by TV standards.*

When Tim turned on the TV this year, Elmer was seated by the large wheel, beaming. Tim checked the board for his best friend George's birthday, May 17th. Number 279. "Lucky bastard," Tim muttered under his breath. "He's ducked it again." Tim and George had worked together at the ad agency until Tim's first unlucky draw. Men with numbers higher than two hundred rarely ended up with a baby at their doorstep.

Tim's birthday, July 19th, had not yet been called.

Now Elmer spun for July 15th. "The lucky number is..." The huge roulette wheel spun, click-clack-click, then stopped at 330.

"Aw, 330!" exclaimed Elmer, disappointed. "That's a high number. Better luck next year."

It annoyed Tim to no end that a high number could be bad. That everyone could be so cheery, so upbeat about low numbers. Changing men's lives forever. It was atrocious!

Curt's yelling distracted Tim for a moment. Then Elmer called out "July 19th." Tim stared at the TV, shaking.

Time stopped. The world slowed down as the wheel clicked, making its way around the large circle. Then it decelerated. All motion stopped. Everything around Tim stopped. The kids stopped yelling. Roger in his crib stopped crying. There was nothing. Nothing. Except... the number... "5."

His heart sank. It couldn't be! "Five! *Five?*"

Tim could barely function. He picked up the phone. "Cindy! Can you come over and cover me here?"

"Sure, Tim." His next-door neighbor was compassionate. She, too, had been watching the Draft, worrying about Tim, fearing he couldn't handle yet another child. She knew he was already on the edge.

Through his mind fog, Tim grabbed a warm coat, put it over his pajamas, and rushed out in his slippers as Cindy came in, facing four screaming kids.

Tim exited the apartment building into the chill of the morning. Standing in the street, he didn't hear a taxi honking as it roared by. "Just run me over," Tim muttered. The next cab stopped, and he jumped in. He gave the driver the address for the agency he'd worked for until the unlucky year when he'd lost the Draft for the first time.

He jumped out of the cab, ran into the building, and took the elevator to the tenth floor. He walked right by Millie, the receptionist.

"Tim? Tim. You can't go in there."

He ignored her and burst into George's office. George, who had never lost the Draft, looked up from his desk. Lucky bastard.

"Did you see? Did you see?" Tim stammered.

"The Draft? I watched until they called my number, then got a phone call and had to get to work. Lucky, huh?" Suddenly, George seemed to become aware of Tim's expression. "Oh... my... God, Tim. What number did you get?"

"Five! Five! I fucking got five! I'm dead, man. I can't do it. I've got Curt driving me crazy. Roger's still in his crib. Number five? Why is there no sense to it? No limits? I called the Center last year after they dropped Roger on my doorstep and screamed at them. 'How can you do this to me?' Do you know what they said? 'Men made the laws that said all fertilized eggs must become babies. These are your rules.'"

"They aren't *my* rules," sobbed Tim. "They're my dad's rules. Not *my* rules."

George looked at Tim with anguish but had no words. All men were powerless in America now.

* * *

**February 28, 2067**

On February 28, it happened. There was a knock on Tim's door. He felt dread, not expecting any visitors except one, the Center for the RTL.

He opened the door reluctantly. A woman stood in the hallway, smiling, accompanied by two others, each holding a bundle.

"You're so lucky! You've got twins!"

Six weeks later, Tim was exhausted. The way he'd been every day since Curt arrived. But he was more than exhausted: drained, shattered, incoherent. He'd spent another day trying to rock the twins and get them to eat. Curt screamed at the top of his lungs. Lucy and Max demanded attention. Roger, Curt, and Max still in diapers in addition to the twins. Finally, Lucy, Max, and Roger were in their beds.

Tim watched the twins, asleep in his arms. He couldn't believe how beautiful they were. It made him so sad. Holding one in each arm, he tiptoed into the bedroom to check that Lucy and Max were asleep. He smiled at Lucy's sweet face, at Max's cuteness. As he entered the babies' room, Roger was asleep in his crib, but when the floor creaked, he awoke. Now all three were crying.

He put the twins down, then went from one crib to the other, trying to soothe them, rubbing their backs. They were still fussing, but Tim, completely beat, left and shut the door to the room, ignoring their cries. Curt was watching TV. Tim knew the boy would either crash in front of the TV for the night or scream around midnight for his dad to get up and take him into their bed. Curt had never been able to sleep in a bed alone.

Tim crept by softly so as not to attract Curt's attention, unlocked the front door, and then headed quietly to the bathroom. He shut the door and telephoned Cindy. "I need your help."

"Sorry, Tim, but it's late. Maybe tomorrow."

"No," he said it quietly, but even he could hear the despair in his tone. "The kids need your help... now. Tomorrow will be too late."

"What's wrong, Tim?"

But Tim couldn't answer. He had slashed his wrists and was bleeding to death on the bathroom floor.

\* \* \*

### Becoming a Grandparent

"Mr. Mitchell?" the policeman on the porch asked.

"Yes?" Mitch Mitchell felt a sense of dread; whatever it was, he knew it wasn't going to be good.

"We are sorry to inform you that your son, Tim, passed away last night."

Mitch was stunned, but he remained stoic. "How?"

"I'm sorry, sir. He committed suicide."

Mitch just stood, shocked. They hadn't been close since Tim drew his first unlucky number in the Draft. His wife, Gloria, had passed away a year after Tim first lost the Draft. She'd never gotten over blaming Mitch for Lizzy's death. Then seeing Tim with a problem child had broken her heart.

Mitch didn't know what to feel. He simply thanked the policeman, who turned and left.

As soon as he was alone, Mitch's phone rang.

"Mr. Mitchell?"

"Yes."

"This is Director Martin from the Center for the Right to Life." The woman's authoritative voice was irritating. "Don't go anywhere. We have paperwork we need you to sign."

"What's this about?"

"Please don't leave, sir. That would cause you legal difficulty. We will be right there."

Click.

Ten minutes later, when he responded to the knock on his door, he saw two black cars parked in front of his Maryland residence. A tall woman with a "Center for the RTL" patch stood on his porch. Mitch looked at her warily. Her nametag said, *Martin*.

"This shouldn't take long, sir. Is there a place we can sit down and review the paperwork?"

"What paperwork?"

"Please, sir, the explanation is in the paperwork. Where can we sit and review it?"

He motioned her to sit on the couch, and he took a chair.

She sat, put her binder down on the coffee table between them, and opened it to the first page.

*Mitchell Adoption*, it read in large bold letters. Suddenly realizing the implications, Mitch felt his eyes grow wide. "I can't... what? What is this?"

"Obviously, sir, your son's unfortunate demise means he can no longer fulfill his obligations to the government to care for his six children."

"Six?" Mitch stammered, then he remembered about the twins.

"Since Tim never legally assigned a godparent, the responsibility falls to you, his father, the children's grandfather."

"No, what? I'm seventy-five years old. I can't take on six children, twin babies."

"Legally, they are your responsibility."

"Take them back to the Center!" he directed.

"That wouldn't be legal," Director Martin answered coldly. She paused, and her voice softened a bit. "I understand this is happening suddenly, but there are no other options. The responsibility is yours and yours alone."

She turned to the signature page in the binder and held out a pen. "Sign," she directed. He looked at the doorway and saw two guards, armed, standing there at attention. He understood. *Take the children or go to jail.* He signed.

She rose and left six folders on the coffee table, each labeled with one of the children's names. The last name on each was Mitchell. "I am sure you will be a good grandparent to the children. But, of course, there are significant fines and legal issues for men who shirk their duty. Oh, and I suggest you identify a godparent. You're getting up there in age." He could see a slight smirk on her face. Then her face softened. "We will bring the children in now. Please greet them warmly. They have been through a lot."

She turned and went to the door. Mitch sat, shocked. He couldn't think straight. Then Lucy and Max ran in with tears in their eyes and hugged him. "Oh, Grandpa. Daddy's gone," little Lucy sobbed. They had only seen their grandfather a few times at Christmas, but they remembered him. Kids do.

Curt walked up and kicked him in the shin.

The children's clothes, toys, diapers, a week's supply of food and formula, and multiple car seats were carried in and set down on the floor. Finally, the twins came, pushed in a double baby carriage.

"This is Inge," Director Martin introduced the tall, gray-haired, Swedish woman, helping Roger toddle in. "She will assist you in making a smooth transition with the children today. It's a new service we offer for the children's sake. She can lend a hand as you prepare lists of how to care and feed them and make school plans. She can stay until the children are in bed tonight and can return during the day tomorrow if you still need her and then offer phone consultations for a week."

He nodded, relieved that he wasn't going to just suddenly be left with them all. "Yes, please."

Inge held Max's and Lucy's hands while Mitch carried a squirming Curt and showed the children their rooms. A staff member set up two cribs, and another staffer carried Roger to one of them and then went back for the twins. Inge began moving their belongings into their rooms.

Director Martin said, "Could I have one more word with you, sir? Alone."

Inge picked up Curt and carried him into the den where Max and Lucy were watching TV, leaving only Director Martin and Mitch in the living room.

"You know, during your time as Congressman, women didn't *want* to make the choice between bearing an unwanted child or having an abortion. Young girls still in high school, women who were raped or with too many children already, women just feeling they had no control over their bodies and their lives. I think men in America now understand how the loss of control feels when the government makes the decisions about your life. I really hope this will work out for you and your grandchildren. They need you. And I am sorry for your loss, sir."

She left and shut the door softly behind her. A tear rolled down his cheek.

*＊ ＊ ＊*

*This story first appeared in the After Dinner Conversation—May 2023 issue.*

## Discussion Questions

1. What do you think would happen if women could easily and cheaply have a newly conceived child removed and grown outside of their body? How do you think society would change?
2. Would you support a law that required men to have a 50/50 chance of being the primary caregiver for the children of all unplanned pregnancies?
3. Assuming there were far more children placed in adoption than those looking to adopt, would you support a "Draft" like the one in the story? Why or why not? Do you have an alternative?
4. Given the choice between easy and inexpensive access to incubated babies, like in the story, and easy and inexpensive access to contraception and abortion, which would you prefer and why?
5. Does the government have a responsibility to provide excellent care for unwanted children? What societal advantages/disadvantages exist in pushing that responsibility onto individuals through a system like the story's "Draft"?

\* \* \*

# For Your Safety

*Ty Lazar*

\*\*\*

"Ms. Ortiz?"

No. It couldn't be.

"Yes?" Zoe's heart started racing.

"Hi there!" The buzz-cut Black woman introduced herself and the faux-hawked white man accompanying her. Their smiles were warm and practiced, their demeanors skillfully casual. "We're from the Department of Public Health. Sorry to bother you so late. May we come in?"

So much for the best stream scrambler on the black market.

"Um—sure."

Zoe was wearing her hookup's T-shirt, which came down to her knees. She couldn't remember his name. Had she asked? Guilt commingled with nerves as she led them into her cramped apartment.

"Are you alone?" Buzz Cut asked.

"Yep," Zoe lied, with what was no doubt a suspicious

adrenaline spike. She wasn't sure why she did it. He hadn't come out of the bedroom yet; maybe he was scared, maybe he wanted to face them alone, when they came knocking on his own door.

She gestured at the kitchen table and the three of them sat down. She felt herself turning red, from anxiety, from anger, and hoped it didn't show, which only made it worse.

"Ms. Ortiz," Buzz Cut started, letting her nonchalance gently fall away, "we're here because we received a notification from your LiveWell stream of a...well..."

"A dopamine spike," Faux Hawk finished softly, his face steeped in sorrowful concern.

Reflexively Zoe glanced at the bedroom, whose door was ajar not fifteen feet away. They didn't seem to notice.

"Now, considering the profile and intensity of the spike," Buzz Cut said, "and the surrounding biochemical signatures—"

"—oxytocin, prolactin—" Faux Hawk added.

"—the evidence is consistent with...well...I think you know what we're getting at." Buzz Cut smiled awkwardly.

Indignation finally overtook the fear, giving Zoe a burst of courage. "Say it," she commanded. Her heart was thumping violently.

Faux Hawk answered, softer and graver than before. "It's a clear instance of sexual climax."

Zoe was burning with rage and resentment and helplessness. She inhaled, then exhaled, then swallowed. She felt herself come down a bit.

"How do you know it wasn't just me?"

"There was somebody in your immediate vicinity whose indicators correlated with yours in a way that...left no doubt." It was Faux Hawk's turn to look awkward.

"Now, we checked our records, Ms. Ortiz," Buzz Cut said, "and, unfortunately, we couldn't find an IPA filed under your name."

Zoe stared blankly.

"IPA stands for Intimate Partnership Agreem—"

"I know what it stands for," Zoe interrupted. "I know," she repeated, more calmly.

"I'm sorry, but we have to ask," Faux Hawk said, and continued in a painfully apologetic tone, his voice rising at least an octave as he spoke: "*Have* you filed an IPA with the department?"

Zoe locked eyes with him for as long as she could bear. "No."

Faux Hawk closed his eyes and nodded tragically. From Zoe's bedroom came a quick succession of sharp, plastic thuds, like something dropping. She stopped herself from jumping, forced herself to breathe evenly.

Her interrogators exchanged glances but said nothing.

Buzz Cut fixed Zoe with a solemn look. "Now, you are aware, Ms. Ortiz, that for your safety and the safety of others, sexual relations are prohibited between individuals who have not entered into an IPA ratified by the Department of Public Health."

"I know that," Zoe sighed. "I know. Look, I didn't plan for it to happen, it was just—things got out of control, and... We used protection. We were careful." She had started off intending to sound defiant but it came out apologetic, groveling, and she hated herself more than she hated the haircuts sitting across from her.

Buzz Cut smiled, her eyes radiating sympathy and

understanding. "I'm very glad to hear that, Ms. Ortiz, and I truly appreciate that you made an effort to look after your health and that of your partner. Thanks to you and so many other diligent people across this country, we've prevented millions of sexually transmitted infections and saved thousands of lives since the reforms. But unfortunately, even with protection, the risk is still present. Lives are still lost. What if—God forbid—you were infected with HIV or hepatitis C and didn't know it, and your protection failed? How would you feel if you unknowingly passed a deadly virus to your partner tonight?"

Zoe glared at Buzz Cut with what she hoped came off as stony indifference. The stress of the past ten minutes had hit her. She wanted these people to do what they had to and leave.

"As public health professionals," Buzz Cut continued, "we understand the benefits of sexual intimacy for mental and physical wellness. But it's just as important to seek out those benefits responsibly, Ms. Ortiz. That's where our department's IPA program comes in. The testing, monitoring, and exclusivity requirements will empower you and your partner to enjoy your relationship safely and with full peace of mind."

Buzz Cut paused. Zoe shifted her gaze somewhere off into space.

"We're not here to scold you, Ms. Ortiz. We're here to help you and educate you." She stood, and her associate, ever in sync, did the same. "This is the first offense on your record, so you'll only receive a fine. But you should be aware that in case of a second offense, the law prescribes a regimen of oxytocin-based empathy enhancement therapy." When Zoe didn't react, Buzz Cut went on: "It's been shown to boost pro-social behavior, including compliance with public health measures designed to keep us all safe."

Zoe's hookup had tried discreetly to swallow a pill tonight, had nearly jumped through the ceiling when she asked about it. Could it be? In her bones she knew the answer. No doubt he was being monitored for the appropriate biomarkers.

"If you and your partner intend to see each other regularly, we urge the two of you to set up an IPA. It's super easy—you can do it through your LiveWell app."

Zoe stared at her lap, waiting. Finally she heard the scraping of chairs, a pair of footsteps, the front door easing open.

"What about the third time?"

Faux Hawk, who was busying himself with his jacket, looked over his shoulder. "Department policy would require us to file a recommendation that three points be deducted from your Social Confidence Rating."

Three points. She'd lose her job. She'd never find work again. The guilt from before ballooned in her chest as she fought another urge to glance at the bedroom.

"Stay safe," Buzz Cut said, but before clicking the door shut behind her she stopped, then pushed it gingerly back open and looked inquiringly at Zoe.

"Is your guest still here, Ms. Ortiz?"

Something flared inside Zoe, wrenching her out of her stupor. She got to her feet. "If you'll excuse me, it's late and I'm tired."

"I understand," Buzz Cut said, "but we'd have to pay him a visit anyway. Wouldn't it be easier for all involved if we took care of it now?"

Something wasn't right. Zoe considered a moment, then

said, "Right now Jake wants to be alone. And so do I."

Suddenly Buzz Cut was back inside the apartment. "Jake?" she yelled to the bedroom. "Mind if we have a quick chat?"

Nobody spoke. The tension stretched the ensuing seconds, then dissipated when it became clear that no answer was coming. Zoe smiled.

"His name's not Jake. Well, maybe it is. I have no idea. We met online two hours ago and he came over and fucked me." It took everything she had to keep her voice from quivering. "I don't know anything about him. And it looks like neither do you."

Buzz Cut opened her mouth as if searching for a reply while Faux Hawk pressed his lips together, looking as though he wanted to melt into the floor.

"Must have an ID spoofer," Zoe said. "Hard to come by, thanks to you people. Might have to see if I can snag one for myself, replace that junk stream scrambler."

"Ms. Ortiz—" Buzz Cut began, moving farther into the apartment, but Zoe cut her off.

"Take another step and you're trespassing."

A beat passed; nobody moved. Faux Hawk looked about to try his own luck at speaking when Buzz Cut rested a hand on his shoulder, and without a word, they left.

Zoe stood rooted to the floor, blood pounding through her body, and breathed. But as the nerves receded, they gave way to a strange unease in the pit of her gut. She grabbed a glass of water from the counter and walked, slowly, to her bedroom, the dread thickening with each step. When she pushed open the door, the glass slipped out of her hand and shattered on the floor.

Tendrils of water slithered out from the shards and coalesced around an empty pill bottle, which lay under the unconscious hand dangling over the edge of the bed.

*  *  *

*This story first appeared in the After Dinner Conversation—December 2021 issue.*

## Discussion Questions

1. Of course, one of the modern roles of government is to create laws that limit freedoms to protect citizens; seat belt laws, smoking laws, etc. Besides tradition, how do you know the distinction between appropriate, and inappropriate, freedom limiting laws for the protection of citizens?
2. You are required to inform someone attempting to buy your house if the house has lead paint, or other unseen issues that might affect their health. Is that different than being required to tell a sexual partner about a sexually transmitted disease?
3. How is a credit score different than a "social confidence rating?" What would be legitimate and illegitimate examples/uses of each?
4. One of the advantages of Uber, Airbnb, or other social trust systems is the ratings. Would you support a voluntary (*or mandatory*) app that allowed someone to rate their interactions with others, or share medical information with potential partners?
5. Like wiretaps or email surveillance, some argue, for those with nothing to hide, government monitoring is meaningless. How are these examples the same, or different types of invasions of privacy for the protection of societal safety?

\* \* \*

# Understanding Ice Cream

*Earl Smith*

\* \* \*

"Class dismissed," Professor Gault said. "Chapters five through nine next time."

As they filed out, the thoughts came. "Another unproductive session. They're graduate students. Years of education. And for what? They should be able to understand the dynamics of political polarization by now. Instead, they get caught in the web. An insect caught in the web is not the spider. By now they should be the spider." He smiled at the idiocy of the thought. "They fall into the trap so easily and get stuck. One side is wrong—misguided—ignorant. And they identify with the side they think holds the high moral ground. Foolishness. Where are the minds that can bridge the chasm?"

Those thoughts followed him out into the quadrangle. It was a pleasant spring afternoon. Mathew decided to forget about the class and the conundrum. He found a vacant bench under a broadly shading tree, sipped his coffee, and vowed to contemplate nature until the clouds cleared.

She entered the quadrangle from the opposite side. He noticed her immediately. Looked to be midsixties. Around five ten, black hair, tanned olive complexion, she walked a measured pace as if in deep contemplation. As that was also his manner, he felt an immediate kinship. "Maybe a visiting professor," he thought. No, the clothes were wrong. Definitely not an American. There was a stylishness about her that American academic women mostly avoided. Faculty frumpy or freaky eccentric is what they opted for these days. He settled on the wife of a visiting donor and turned back to avoiding his conundrum. His miserably unsuccessful efforts to leave it behind were turning into a rout. It leered back at him from an impenetrable mist.

"You seem to be a man with a problem," she said. He hadn't noticed her approaching nor when she sat down at the opposite end of the bench. On closer inspection, her face was perfectly symmetrical. Her eyes were dark, almost black, matching the color of her hair. There was a presence about her that he found mildly disconcerting.

"I'm getting absent-minded," he said. "Or maybe it's the early stages of senility. I'm sorry. I didn't notice you sitting down. It's such a beautiful day. I've decided to play hooky from my..." He paused, not sure how to describe it. "I've not seen you around before. Are you new to the university?"

"You might say that," she said with a gentle smile. "My name is Anna. And it is a lovely day for playing hooky. But you do not seem to be fully enjoying it. I sense that something is troubling you. My father says that talking about such things to a stranger can sometimes clear the way. So, if you are willing to take a chance, tell me what is bothering you."

"Well, let's see if your father is right," he said with a smile. "You're correct. I'm teaching an advanced seminar on contemporary political dynamics. The participants are doctoral and master's students. So, they're not neophytes. They can't seem to think about polarization without getting caught in its snare. It's frustrating. I spend time muttering about spiders and webs. And end up getting nowhere."

"Well, dichotomies are a debilitating distraction dismembering much of what passes for human thought," she said with a sly grin. "What is your area of research?"

"Sociology and politics."

"So, you study the human condition from the perspective of sociology?" she asked.

"You could put it that way, yes. But I limit my focus to the human condition as it engages in politics. It's my calling. And my tormentor. If humans can't teach other humans about such things, then all of this," he said sweeping his hand around the quadrangle, "is just a kamikaze raid on a vacant lot."

"Clearly all of this, as you refer to it, has brought major benefits to humanity," Anna responded. "The question is, does any of it help you with your conundrum? Or is it a straitjacket that keeps you from a new understanding? What was the focus of the seminar?"

"The tabled question was, 'Why are we so polarized?' For two hours there were the standard ruminations on the subject, accompanied by hardening positions on opposite sides. They even got polarized about the definition of polarization."

"They were not polarized," she softly said.

Her statement barely registered. Polarization was the current filet mignon of political theory. Without it, nothing in the contemporary doctrines made any sense. "Not another amateur," he thought to himself.

"I am not the amateur you think I am," she said with a slight smile. He looked at her sharply. "Perhaps I can assist you in ways you might not anticipate. You see polarization as conflict. But let us posit that there are at least two flavors of conflict. One, to use a theological example, is between two who believe in God differently. Both have accepted the existence of a superior being but differ in the description and proscriptions of their deity. A second is between one who worships God and another who does not believe that such an entity exists. You might agree that the nature of these two conflicts is fundamentally different. Atheists are unlikely to attack believers simply because they believe, unless attacked first for nonbelieving. On the other hand, it is far more likely that believers will attack those who, through their heretical beliefs, either misinterpret or misrepresent their God."

Gault turned toward her. "I'll admit I was thinking you are an amateur, but this suddenly seems a conversation worth having. I'll posit there's a difference, but I'm not sure where that takes us. How can you say they were not polarized? It's so obvious that this entire society is polarized. Just look at the political situation. Left against right, men against women, liberals against progressives, conservatives against Trumpsters. Polarization is a defining characteristic of American society."

"Accurate as far as it goes," she replied. "But there is a problem with your analysis. It started with paragraph two. Suppose for a moment that something more fundamental is the defining characteristic of American society."

"What the hell does that mean?" he replied. After a pause, he continued. "I apologize. I didn't mean to respond that way. It's a jarring suggestion. What am I missing?"

"You have ignored the possibility that what you call polarization is simply various manifestations of a defining underlying condition. That polarization is a collection of symptoms of a commonly shared, pervasive disease."

"Go on," he said.

"Do you like ice cream? Chocolate or vanilla?"

The questions stopped him for a bit. He decided to play along. "Yes, I do like ice cream. Almost everybody does. Of the two choices, I prefer vanilla."

"And your students, do they all prefer vanilla as well?"

"I seriously doubt it. They are likely as polarized on this question as they are on political matters. But you seem to be making my case rather than yours."

"So, which is the more defining question? What is the cause of the almost unanimous taste for ice cream, or why do people choose between alternative flavors?"

Gault paused. Then said slowly, "It depends on what part of the process you are focusing on."

"A fair response. But, if you do not answer the first question usefully, how edifying will your answer to the second one be? If you do not understand the conditions that support the urgency that underlies polarization, then how do you find meaning in its various manifestations?"

"You've lost me," Gault said.

"You said that almost everybody likes ice cream," Anna continued. "So, you accept the possibility that, because of an allergy, lactose intolerance, or just a dislike of the taste or texture, there are people who do not get far enough along to make the choice between chocolate and vanilla. Are these the only nonpolarized ones when it comes to ice cream? And how many might suffer from one or more of these conditions and still crave the stuff? Or what of those who are indifferent when it comes to choosing? What does polarization mean within the broader context of preference or a lack thereof?"

Gault looked at her, smiled, and said, "I'm getting the feeling that either a psychiatrist or a philosopher might be handy about now."

"Perhaps," she replied with a playful grin. Gault scratched his chin in thought. Anna continued. "Preference is not prejudice, partisanship, or polarization. It is simply an indicator of a choice from among options. And the needs to make those choices are simply manifestations of the basic underlying condition of liking ice cream and the availability of a range of flavors to choose from."

"I think I'm catching up a bit," he said. "You're suggesting that the disposition toward ice cream is the underlying driver of the choice between flavors? I'll buy that. But aren't those voluntary choices based on individual preferences?"

"You need to go deeper into it," she said. "If you begin with the question, why does one person prefer vanilla over chocolate, without first focusing on the roots of the liking of ice cream, you end up studying the various symptoms of 'liking ice cream.' You are overlooking the underlying condition that makes choosing an imperative."

He started to say something, but Anna raised a hand. "Let me finish the thought. The challenge is that foundational conditions provide a context within which choices are made. Without understanding that underlying context, choices can appear irrational and chaotic."

"Let's follow your reasoning," he said. "What is the underlying condition—the equivalent of liking ice cream—that is driving polarization?"

"Narcissism," she replied. "Intense self-involvement. Hubris. The determinative hegemony of ego. A population of narcissists will always become increasingly polarized as their condition deepens. It is inevitable."

"Are you suggesting that the defining characteristic of my students is a mental disorder?"

"I am suggesting that narcissism is *the* defining characteristic of American contemporary culture. It is the dynamic that is producing an increasingly dysfunctional society. That is because advancing narcissism causes a major internal conflict. Narcissism runs counter to a basic human need. Millions of years of evolution have produced extraordinarily successful social animals. But narcissism produces individuals who are self-definers of truth and fact. The so-called post-truth, post-fact generations. Their mantra is that every individual gets to define what they take to be true as true.

"But the individual isolated and bound within their own insistence on personal sovereignty still feels the need for social context. A truth that cannot be redefined away. The major cause of increasing polarization is the intensifying internal conflicts which arise because of the tensions between advancing narcissism and the echoing needs of an intensely social species."

"Then you are saying that we are all narcissists," came an irritated grumble.

She sighed deeply, then continued, "Narcissism is one of three mental disorders widely seen as untreatable. The others being psychopathy and paranoia. You don't cure a narcissist. To misuse Kierkegaard, such a condition, once reached, is a sickness unto death. But the death of far more than the individual *being qua being*. Once narcissism flowers, the real world dies for the narcissist. A virtual world takes its place."

She turned toward him and said, "Narcissism involves extreme selfishness, a sense of entitlement, a lack of empathy, and a dominating need to be admired. The narcissist sees herself as the center of the universe. Indeed, its very reason for existence. Things such as truth, facts, virtues, and heresies are defined within her driving need to be the essence of every issue, circumstance, event, and thought. She has swallowed the lie that reality can be bent to her claim of omnipotence and omniscience. Her life becomes a fiction based on self-deception."

Anna smiled and asked, "So, what would a society of narcissists look like? How would they find a balance between their narcissistic tendencies and the need for social and cultural context? How would they balance the virtual understanding of their own sovereignty with their real needs for social connections?"

They sat in silence for a while. "Welcome to the void," Anna finally said. "Let us leap in. They would attempt to solve the dilemma by inverting the conditions. A narcissist redefines their virtual sovereignty as reality. Then creates a virtual social context which they also claim to be real. The hope being that these virtual associations will satisfy their need for human connections. But, as the old saying goes, only a fool attempts to warm herself before a picture of a fire."

He looked at her and, almost pleadingly, said, "As I understand it, you are suggesting that a culture of simplemindedness, of the undefined, of indefiniteness, is the only possible outcome in a population of narcissists. That's a..."

Anna interrupted him, smiling impishly, "You know, one of the greatest charlatans of all western philosophers was René Descartes. He famously wrote, *cogito ergo sum*. Roughly translated, 'I think, therefore I am.'"

Mathew grimaced and said, "You are going to suggest that he was wrong, aren't you?"

"Not so much wrong," she replied. "Descartes stopped short for lack of courage. Should he have had the courage, it would have been 'I think I think therefore I am.' And that would have become, 'I think I think therefore I think I am.' And on to, 'I think I think I think therefore I think I am. I think I think I think therefore I think I think I am. I think I think I think I think therefore I think I think I think I am.' And so on, right down the rabbit hole. He said nothing really. And the world found it profound. But he did lay the foundation for the evolution of a narcissism based on simple-minded self-definition. To think you think is to murder the very thing that is thinking. Its connotative substitute is really nothing but a hymn to self-glorification. But this is getting too heavy for such a nice spring afternoon. Let's get back to ice cream."

Gault frowned and shook his head slowly. "If I've followed you, you seem to be suggesting that the inevitable end product of the Age of Reason and the Enlightenment is a population of raving narcissists."

"You are envisioning wandering bands of rabid

vampires," she said. "Reacting without reason. Changing identity on a whim. Drinking their own blood. But that is not what is happening. They are humans choosing virtual sides in a virtual world. Alone, isolated, disconnected except through their gossamer virtual imaginings. Unable to erase the manufactured self at the center of their manufactured universe. They live their lives inside video games in which they are the sole hero. The savior of mankind. If you are going to understand them, you need to muster the courage to step inside that game."

"I would be forever lost," Gault said. "I would cease to exist as the person that I have labored so many years to become. My knowledge is hard won. There is a core of my being that is substantial and real. I need to remain who I am. I've dedicated all my will and knowledge to educating new generations. I cannot do that as a figment of my own imagination."

"If you lack the courage to go further, dedication is a fine palliative. But, at minimum, you need to recognize that your students are doing the only thing that narcissists can do under their circumstances. Making choices that are trivial and claiming them to be foundational."

"They are self-virtualized prophets of their own imagined immortality," Gault said slowly and sadly.

Anna said sharply, "A population of narcissists, all of whom take themselves as prophets of the truth, constitute a legion of false prophets who are morbidly aware of their heresy and their corruption."

Gault felt a panic rush through him. "So, you are saying that a realization that salvation is not coming is driving the behavior of my students? Because they sit upon the throne of a god they have displaced and then denied. They know that it doesn't matter what is called true because they realize their own corruption is the very definition of who they are."

Anna nodded slowly. "Narcissism is a cold and lonely place. The God who has been overthrown cannot be recalled. The god enshrined in his place is a gossamer illusion. The narcissist fears the fate of a false prophet. He who follows the anti-Christ is forever banned from heaven. Condemned eternally to the pit. And the narcissist is both anti-Christ and ardent follower."

After a while, Mathew said. "I always thought I was the sane one, and they, my students, were deluded. But you seem to be suggesting that they are more creatures of their time and aware of their circumstances than I am. That they are the realists and I the... I don't know what I am in that."

"You are mostly irrelevant to them in their attempt to create sanity out of a completely insane situation," Anna said softly.

She reached out and touched his hand. "I am deeply sorry that our conversation has upset you. Please believe me that it was not my intention to spoil this beautiful spring afternoon. But, as jarring as the idea is, there is some merit in considering it."

"I'm not sure I understand what you are getting at, but I suspect I won't like it much if, and when, I do," Gault said.

"Who is the believer and who is the atheist?" she asked. "To you, they are the heretics. They defame your god of reason. Your urgency is to recall the fallen. But your students inhabit a different universe. In Virtual Land, they form armies, identify allies and enemies, assault those who misrepresent their god in battles beyond the stars."

"If my god is reason, what is theirs?" Gault asked.

"Themselves. Each themselves. Alone, isolated, like stars scattered across the void. Emptiness surrounds them and stands between them and any others. They strive to do what all stars must do. Burn brightly and then expire."

"But they don't burn brightly," Gault said. "There is little in them that speaks of brilliance or vision. Only a pedestrian, plodding mindlessness. How is that burning bright?"

"You are looking at it through your eyes," Anna responded. "Try it this way. Suppose you are a narcissist and the self-anointed creator of your world. But the hunger is inside you for social context—a hunger which requires you to recognize others as necessary to your wellbeing. And that thought has brought you to a despair that cannot be willed away. What would you do? How would you act? Would you not want desperately to be famous for even a few hours? Even if it means slaughtering a dozen children with an assault rifle. Or loudly proclaiming that the entire world is corrupt."

"Look at their world through their eyes? I'm not sure I can. The world you describe is so different from mine."

"Then let us focus on an inflection point. You begin to suspect that you are not in control. The arsenic of narcissism. You cannot build and maintain relationships with friends as equals. That path is closed off to you. So, what do you do? You lash out at the insanity of your situation. Rage at the darkness, to borrow a phrase. You manufacture a virtual reality in which you are supreme above all others. Even those who profess to believe all the virtual things you believe are inconveniences bordering on personal insults to your existence."

Anna settled back and then almost whispered, "But your

actions cannot open you to yet another demonstration of your irrelevance and impotence. So, you choose to focus your rage where you are least likely to be proven wrong. What would be more appropriate than politics? You cannot be incorrect. You cannot be denied."

"Are you suggesting that they choose politics because whatever they profess to believe doesn't matter?"

"In a way. Because it allows both meaningless omnipotence and irrelevant omniscience. A narcissist's nirvana."

"You are suggesting that nothing that I am trying to accomplish matters."

Anna leaned forward. "There are impactful political actors. They shape, for better or worse, the arc of human history. But none of your students are likely to become members of that group. They like to think of themselves as the headlining performer at a global concert. But each is more likely to be the occupant of the cheap seat sold at a discount to fill the arena. Irrelevancy is the reality that a narcissist must most ardently deny."

She paused to let her last comment sink in. "Politics is the ideal focus for a narcissist," Anna said. "They can talk about big things without any risk. Nothing will ever come from their ruminations and gnashing of teeth in a world that they fervently avow does not exist—nor in the virtual one they ardently envision. They can strut about, loudly proclaiming their fierce independence. Posturing as the decider of things strategic. Pronouncing definitively. It does not matter which side they take. Vanilla or chocolate, their choice does not matter."

Anna paused, glanced at Gault, and then continued.

"What is necessary for them is an impotent opposition to their claim of omnipotence. And this they decree without fear. They need others to shout, just as ardently and insubstantially, chocolate to their vanilla. Their desire is for an unending, and unresolvable, series of virtual battles beyond the stars against those who misrepresent their god. The legions of vanilla against the hordes of chocolate. Within the cocoon of their fantasies, they take the blue pill and settle into oblivion. To quote Morpheus, 'You take the blue pill... you wake up in your bed and believe whatever you want to believe.' Virtual empowerment. Virtually meaningless."

Anna looked directly into his eyes. "You see, Professor Gault, it really does not matter which side your students take. Chocolate or vanilla. It is all the same choice. Polarization is simply a ploy in a virtual game they play. A manifestation of advancing narcissism. A symptom of the underlying disease."

She glanced at her watch. "I need to be going. I have enjoyed our conversation and hope you have as well."

He shook his head. "Let me see if I understood you. Before there is ice cream, there is no choosing. But, once there is, choosing is only the result of the compelling need to choose. Narcissism compels a choice. In fact, it demands it if the narcissist is to maintain themselves at the center of their worldview. It's the act of choosing, not the actual choice, that is the symptom of the underlying disease. You said, vanilla or chocolate, it really doesn't matter. There is no logic. Only the imperative of choosing. If that is true, what is there for me to do? Have I nothing to contribute?"

"The delusion of pontificating definitively is the defining currency of narcissism," Anna replied. "A narcissist can only maintain their claim to the throne of the overthrown God by self-certifying both omnipotence and omniscience."

"As for your question," Anna said softly, "do as you must. There is nothing more for you than that. Except perhaps a chance of a clearer understanding. There is no exit from your circle of beliefs. Nor any for your students from theirs. To quote an old Zen proverb, '*If you understand, things are just as they are. If you do not understand, things are just as they are.*'"

As she was walking away, Anna paused, glanced back, and said, "By the way, I have never tasted ice cream nor had to choose. Our talk has left me curious."

He watched her cross the quad and disappear through the arch.

*\* \* \**

*This story first appeared in the After Dinner Conversation—March 2023 issue.*

## Discussion Questions

1. How would you summarize the argument that Anna is making about the students, and do you agree with her?
2. Anna argues the underlying trait of the students driving their political debates is their narcissism. Do you agree? What is driving their narcissism?
3. Do you agree with the premise of the story, that narcissism is the foundational trait of political polarization, and that the polarization is the result, regardless whether you are liberal or conservative?
4. If, as Anna proposes, narcissists are fighting an "unending, and unresolvable, series of virtual battles beyond the stars against those who misrepresent their god," then how do you ever stop the cycle of polarization? Do you agree with Anna that once narcissism takes hold the imagined world can never be let go?
5. Do you agree with Anna's supposition that narcissists focus on politics because they want to "focus their rage where they are least likely to be proven wrong"? Are there counterarguments you would like to have made to Anna that the Mathew did not?

\* \* \*

# Prohibition

*David Rose*

\* \* \*

It had been ten days since my last fix.

I knew what I was going to do was wrong, but unless you knew the yearning that your body exerts, the internal pull which strangles your very soul into submission, then you cannot judge me. Yes, it was wrong. Yet that was always so simple to say, to let the word slip from your lips and forget its inability to exist in our world as a proper description. Of course it was wrong. It was also necessary. I knew it was wrong, but I wanted it and I wanted it more and more each meter that I neared. I was not proud, but that didn't mean I didn't like doing what I was going to do. People always want black and white, it comforts them, but I'm not going to give you that. That's too easy.

The electric autotaxi drew to a halt in a derelict, abandoned part of town. The drop in population had left large parts of the city uninhabited and soon the life had been sucked out of them. What was once so human about the world decayed and shriveled when left untouched, leaving nothing but the reminder – the echo – of the image of man. Yet, it was no longer human, structures neither alive nor dead.

The computerized voice informed me of the fare. I swept my debit card through the magnetic slot on the console and waited for the network to authorize the payment. "Thank you, Mr. Bronte," the flat, impersonal tone reminding me that it was no longer possible to hide, to disappear; making sure I knew that every movement of my life was tracked. I had made sure I still had a walk to reach my destination, but the nagging which was worse than guilt shook its head behind my back; the disapproval of an almost omniscient power which believed in the certainty of its judgment.

I placed my hand on the door which exhaled smoothly. As I stepped out, I heard the inevitable Japanese-accented Americanism: "Have a nice day, Mr. Bronte." Christ, who wrote the software for these machines? The singular was always being squeezed out by the criterion of cost-effectiveness: why adapt it, when people will just learn from it?

It was a dark winter evening; frosty, the breeze crisp. The taxi hummed as it pulled away to another call or to circle the night streets. I waited until it turned a corner, then I doubled back on myself and set off, my body being rushed by pumping desire.

I turned quickly left and shuffled into the dark away from the neon blue streetlights. The alley was narrow, the light made a vain attempt to penetrate but quickly retreated, defeated. I could make out the dark shapes of industrial bins and dumped rubbish. The empty familiarity was soothing, a promise to my aching want: this was the right place because there was no one and no one was mockingly whispered in the rush of the wind.

I pulled my collar tight around me. The guilt followed me, amusing me, the wrong an ecstasy without an erection; flesh without penetration. The urge began to speak to me now, telling me of its wants, how it would repay me with absolute pleasure rushing through my veins. Promised heaven, if only I did what it wanted. Addiction.

Those who craved black and white loved this word. Physical, or psychological, at least it was an explanation. An explanation which put an expanding abyss between them and me; I was unfortunate, but they could never, never be like me. I was addicted and needed help: poor, poor me. Save me!

I smile to myself. They understand nothing. I am the same as you, I am you. It's an addiction because – and this is the thing you fear most – I like doing it. My tongue has an erection just thinking about it, my blood rushes in preparation. My body and I, both of us, want it because it is pleasant. That's the bottom line. That's why I'm here. Again. And, that's why I'll be back in the future, because it is good to do.

Silence gently lapped about me as I paced towards the hidden, steel door. I knew this place, I knew the dealer personally. I was a regular and this, in this countercultural underground, was important. It meant trust. And trust made a difference. None of that mixed shit sold to the unsuspecting. Shit which could have you vomiting for a week. No bad cuts. Here I could be certain that I was buying what they told me. I could afford such a luxury, I was lucky. When I pass the thin, pale skeletons on the streets, clutching their stomachs as though torn in two, I remind myself just how lucky the wealthy are. We can afford to indulge our desires.

I stopped in front of the door, hidden to all who did not know. A sheet of mirrored steel nailed to the wall. I took my mobile out and pressed the memory key which sent the pre-set text message. I waited twenty seconds and my phone rang. I brought the screen level with my face so they could see who I was. I could see no one, as I expected.

"Good evening, Jack."

"Good evening," I responded to my phone.

"Are you alone?"

I passed the vidiphone over my shoulder and turned it through three hundred and sixty degrees. The line cut off abruptly.

Another twenty seconds and the door was slowly pushed open. I stepped back to avoid it and then quickly entered. Inside was another door at the base of the basement stairs, a restaurant with that ubiquitous sign for the initiated: "Quality Red Wine". I felt at home as though a cleaver had divided me from those who did not know, and its clean cut had made the reason for pretense disappear. Warmth entered my body, it relaxed slightly. Satisfaction was near. I was amongst my own people now, those who crawled under the blustery clichés carried by middle English voices.

I descended the stairs and pulled the entrance open.

"Good evening, Mr. Bronte," the large man greeted me.

"Hello, Jerome," I said. "Are you busy tonight?"

"Just you and one other client."

"Good, I like privacy," I responded.

"Please follow me. It is good to see you after such a brief time."

A brief time. I had been coming more often it was true,

but I had just been promoted at work. A thirty percent increase, I could afford a little self-indulgence now. Not only that, but now it would be only the best places with the best cuts. Christ I'm fortunate, I have my habit – as my mother so delicately describes it when talking about other people oblivious to her own son's problem – but, at least, I don't need to take risks. There were diseases out there. Jerome and his mock civility were a price worth paying.

We walked through the set tables, candles acting as beacons to light our way, our steps silenced by the plush, dark, red carpet. Jerome pulled the seat out for me and I sat. He was ludicrously large for a waiter, but we all knew the reason for that. I looked about and noticed the other diner. A woman, herself alone, yet I had no desire to join her. We were here to indulge ourselves, what we were to do was necessarily antisocial. I couldn't see what she was taking, but she had obviously started. Her eyes were closed, in rapture, her head swaying dancing to some internal, secret tune.

I was jealous. I wanted mine now. But, I was aware there were still several rounds of the game to play.

Jerome came back and placed a bottle of Tuscan red on the table. He was unenthusiastic, he knew me, but even counter is a culture. His fingers were tightly wrapped around the neck of the bottle. I said nothing. I knew the rules. Jerome departed leaving the wine on the table.

I remembered my first time, how green I had been. When the bottle had been placed on my table, I had protested and said I didn't order it. The bottle had gone, as had any chance of ever ordering. It had taken three weeks of choosing from the normal menu to learn the rules of the game.

I pulled a corkscrew out of my pocket and placed it in the bottle. I pushed a button and it hummed to itself as it slowly opened the bottle. When I had passed the first test, I had fucked up in asking the waiter to open the bottle for me. If you wanted it, you opened the bottle yourself. A small price to pay. I poured myself a healthy glass of the deep, heavy red. It coated my throat, promising that ecstasy which was to come.

Jerome was once more at my table. He handed me the menu. I perused it quickly. The normal dishes jarred on my retina: creamed asparagus tagliatelle, artichoke risotto, and so on. My blood froze, my desire waited, "I'm sorry, Jerome, but does the chef have any specials tonight?"

"Well, he has a choice between new potatoes with fresh mint, and garden vegetables served with horseradish sauce."

"I'll take the garden vegetables."

Jerome bowed, took the menu and walked off towards the kitchen.

It was done. God, it felt good. Exciting. I had done it a thousand times and each one was a rush. Doing wrong and enjoying it. The wait. The want. I could taste it now. To be honest, I liked the game. It gave the sin meaning.

The plate arrived before me. Jerome smiled, "A special for a regular."

I couldn't believe it, it was on the bone. Flesh, red like the wine, succulent like the body of my first love. I looked up at Jerome as he passed me the knife with teeth, the illegal, outmoded knife. He nodded and moved away.

Slowly, tenderly, I cut into the beef and gazed at the thin line of blood which oozed on to the white, innocent plate. I watched it encircle the joint before raising the meat to my mouth. I placed it gently on my tongue.

The ecstasy.

I sighed. Christ, I was lucky to have found this place. Its name had been passed on to me via the grapevine, but since the first time I had come here, I had made it my main supplier. I could afford to, not many could. The shit they had given me in other places: cut with fifty percent soya, diseased, stuff that would have you vomiting for weeks. In some places, they even tried to fob chicken off on you. Bastards: a meat so bland, I had been surprised that the government had decided to ban it. (It still only carries a sentence of just six months.) Here, I was sure that the meat was genuine. On good days cow, horse and sheep. Bad days, pigeon, gull or hedgehog.

Other meat eaters were always nostalgic, it was better in the good old days for them. I disagree, I like the whole, odd ritual, but then I am younger than them. They are old enough to get away with talking about it in public. I remembered my grandfather, staunchly one of the very last, proudly defying the picket line at the butcher's. The small, cold, damp packet tucked under his arm, he would turn to their cries of "Murderer!" and tell them, slowly but with the dignity of the righteous and the expert wit to appeal to my six-year-old sense of humor, "Fuck off, you wankers."

I liked the old butchers, but not for its clinical white walls or its smell of disinfectant, or even the empty counter which seemingly sold nothing. No, I loved going there because I'd always ask, "What's this place, granddad?" He would turn to me and answer simply, "Civilization."

When my mother found out, she never spoke to her father again. Just for buying something which, then, wasn't even illegal. I was never allowed to even speak about visiting "that place." I remembered my mother's tears when she learnt that her father had been killed outside "that place." Two years later they passed the law.

I placed another piece on my mouth. The blood ran down my tongue as my teeth penetrated the flesh. I swallowed. Pleasure. Heaven. Forbidden. I put down the cutlery and picked the bone up. I caressed it. I looked around. No one. The barbarism of what I was about to do disgusted me, yet I couldn't stop myself. No one. I could do it, I was the sole judge of my actions.

I bit at the meat like a man possessed. The lust of the maniac, the call of the savage. Me as I should be, free of society's false dictates.

I tore at the bone and at the instant I could not believe we were given teeth for any other purpose. Voracious, the drives of the beast in my true soul cried out and I sated them. Each bite was satisfaction, each tear with my teeth, a release. In my hidden, dark corner, I rolled the joint over and over in my greasy, fat fingers. Juice dribbled down my chin, and I almost laughed with joy. I ate like an animal because I was an animal, and the ritual was almost as exciting as the flavor.

Then, came the banging and the shouting.

I put the joint nervously down. I wiped my hands. More voices. I pulled my coat off the back of the chair and slipped my arms into it. Something was happening, I could hear the voices growing louder outside.

Then, nothing.

The silence was more ominous. I took a deep mouthful of wine, waiting, expectant. No place could stay secret forever. Cold sweat ran down the side of my body. Another mouthful of wine, almost the whole glass. They said they could smell the flesh on your breath, and see the blood in your eyes.

The other diner stood. She began walking to the door.

Suddenly, the door smashed open. Jerome rolled over and over. His head lifted up and I saw the blood running swiftly from his nose.

Fear stabbed me like a skewer. I smelt death, the thick, congealed stench of blood. I blew the candle out, swept the plate from the table and threw myself to the floor. I put the table in order and hid myself in the space between the back of the chair and the wall. My breathing ceased, cut short.

I sat still and waited. An eternity unfolded. The door slowly swung open once more. Two pairs of polished black boots entered. Police, I knew it at once. The fucking pigs. I wanted to scream out, to run, to shout. I didn't, I stayed still and silent.

I was in serious trouble now. If they found me, it would be two years in prison or, worse, becoming an informer for life. Either way, I'd lose my job, my credit; my friends would look on me like a piece of shit. Some of the more liberal ones would try – desperately – to understand my illness. A life of constant rehabilitation, of perpetual confession and guilt in the presence of others. I'd probably have to appear on one of the daytime holoshows with a caption defining me as 'I eat flesh and blood.' Fuck, things were looking bad.

I turned slightly. I could see more than their boots now. Jerome was tied to a chair, his head sunk into his chest. The woman was being handcuffed into a chair next to him, they both had their backs to me. The policeman was in his late fifties, about ten years older than me, and was muttering to himself and shouting every third word.

I couldn't see the other policeman. Panic gripped me. My body shrank, trying to disappear in a vortex.

I heard his voice, "The kitchen's empty, sarge. The butcher must have legged it, there was a window open on the back alley."

The sarge replied, "Let him go, he'll be gone by now. Check the rest of the place."

A wide torch beam swept over the restaurant. I heard footfalls near my table and I saw his boots out of the corner of my eye. Please. He stopped, I remained taut. The ray of light swung back and forward like a pendulum.

He walked away and faced Jerome. He was younger than his colleague. "Only the one ghoul tonight, just this bitch, eh?"

The torch smashed into Jerome's face. His face fell deeper into his chest, his voice was weak: "Don't know, I just stand by the door. Don't take it myself, it disgusts me."

The sarge put an arm on his younger colleague. "Easy, we'll just call for backup."

"It's just they fucking disgust me, these fucking cannibals. Christ, can't you smell the stench, it makes you want to vomit."

The sarge took his mobile out, but the younger one stopped him.

"Wait, Sarge. Maybe we can get some info out of him. You know I want to be a detective, give me a chance."

The sarge looked dubious, but after two seconds put his phone back in its holster, he began walking to the kitchen: "You've got ten minutes, then I'm calling it in."

He turned back to Jerome when the sarge had left the room, his eye the embodiment of evil ambition, "So, you don't do it, then?"

Jerome stuttered, "No, I'm just the hired muscle."

The policeman scoffed, "So, Mr. Muscle, how come only the one junkie tonight?"

"Midweek, always quiet."

Jerome's whole body slumped, I saw it fall in on itself as the torch came down on his head. The policeman's face was rage. He lifted Jerome by the chin and let go. His heavy head fell and rocked twice.

The copper turned to the woman. She was sobbing, the sound of fear carried clearly to my ears. Jerome was mumbling incoherently.

"Never mind, Mr. Muscle, we'll come back to you." His eyes turned psychotically on the woman, "He doesn't do it. He's no junkie, he's just hired help. That I can forgive, but," his voice was rising, out of control, the will of ingrained hate, "you, on the other hand. You, you are fucking scum!"

She screamed. He slapped her. Hard. Part of me wanted to run to her defense. My body stayed still. Quiet. It curled even more tightly.

"See, I would like a little help, I need to know where else you buy this shit and who from." A second slap. "Will you tell me that?"

She was crying now. Screaming hysterically, spitting and sobbing.

"Tell me," he repeated.

More sobbing, less words. He shook her, her chair tapping mercilessly on the wooden floor.

"Listen, you disgusting whore. You flesh-sucking bitch. I want to know where you get your vile little habit seen to, understand? I want some info!"

Nothing, more tears, more screams.

He slapped her again, his voice was neurotic, obsessive, "You disgust me. Why are you crying? Have you never heard an animal whine, bitch? They cry just like you – you don't care about that, why should I care about you, eh? My boy's got a new puppy, that's just fodder for people like you, isn't it? I suppose you would fucking chop it up, wouldn't you? You make me sick!"

He spat in her face. Twice. Silence, then the screaming. So loud this time, his colleague came running back in: "What have you done?"

The pig wasn't listening, "Is it meat you want? You want meat whore? Do you want my meat, eh? Do you want to eat that? Shut up! Stop screaming."

I was immobile, watching the smart, polished black boots circled the chair. I did nothing as those clean, blue sleeves pushed down on her shoulders. I was petrified as the smooth, shiny baton was raised into the air.

And then I heard the smack.

Silence.

"What the fuck?" Jerome stammered, still not fully conscious as the line of blood whipped across his face.

I was gripping the legs of the chairs. My nails had broken on its wood. The two pigs were silent.

Then, the younger one pushed her chair over and began kicking her corpse. Kick after kick, he was sobbing as he tried to shout at her, "You disgust me. You disgust me! It's not normal, it's not fucking human. Whore!"

I could feel myself trembling, but I was fixed, I wasn't able to look away. I wanted to flee, but the scene held me, reflecting what could have been and still may have been. Paralyzed, I was nailed to the floor.

The sarge pulled him off, one last kick landing on her inert head, lifting it into the air rocking like a battered apple on a branch.

"Calm down, mate. Calm down. It's alright."

Then, he realized, "Shit, what have I done, Sarge? What have I done? My career is finished."

His partner had walked to the body and was lightly touching her neck, "You've killed her."

"Shit!"

"Well, she's no fucking loss to humanity," the sarge opined philosophically. "Scum like her is better off dead. I'd kill the whole fucking lot of them, given a choice. Fucking junkie vampires."

The sarge turned her body over to take a closer look, "She hasn't bled too much."

"So?"

"So, we can save your career. Be a shame to waste it because of scum like her." He unlocked her hands and began lifting the body. "Help me. We'll throw her in the alley where the chef scampered; it'll only be another dead body. They'll find evidence of flesh in her stomach, they'll assume it was a gangland job. Not paying her dues."

"Are you sure?"

"Yes," the sarge replied, "they find twenty dead bodies a day in this city. They're too busy to go too deep. Come on and help me if you want a job tomorrow."

"You're right. No one cares about one more corpse nowadays. What about him, though?"

They both looked at Jerome. He shriveled up in their gaze.

The sarge put the corpse down and neared Jerome menacingly: "He won't say anything, will you?"

Jerome was shaking his head violently. I felt my own head involuntarily shake from side to side.

The sarge raised his hand. Jerome closed his eyes. The pig took out Jerome's wallet. He took the ID card and scanned it into his palmtop.

And his cuffs were undone.

"We know who you are and where you live. We know your mobile number and your ID. If you talk, not only do you have to explain you're a bouncer at a meat factory, but – remember! – we'll find out and we can trace you anywhere, okay?"

Jerome nodded. He stood up. He looked around. Fear. What was he looking for? What was he doing? My flesh began to crawl tight across my back. Jerome blinked twice, a trapped animal. He ran swiftly out of the door.

The pigs picked the corpse up together. "Christ you can smell the stench in her blood, fucking ghoul," I heard one of them almost spit. They swayed into the kitchen and I heard the backdoor slam.

I waited, shivering under the table, for about half an hour. I crawled out, blinking like a rabbit on the autoway. My eyes shot from shadow to shadow.

I ran into the toilets, they were on the opposite side to the kitchen, and pulled myself through the small, ground-level window.

The night was black and the damp air had descended. I pulled my coat tightly about me. I should walk a couple of miles before hailing a taxi, I didn't want my credit rating to place me in this zone tonight. Shit, what a nightmare.

Soon, the sun would be rising. Already, though, I could feel that insatiable, inhuman longing rising within me. Reason would argue for a while, but ultimately lose. The sickening desire was still deep inside me, driving me on. For now, I could repress it. But I was not certain for how long I could keep the beast within me chained.

I walked into the cold, fresh slap of the dawning human world.

*\*\*\**

*This story first appeared in the After Dinner Conversation—September 2021 issue.*

## Discussion Questions

1. The police seem to have very little respect for the "addicts." Does what they are addicted to change how you view the police officers' actions? What if the addicts had been drug addicts? Cannibals? Child pornographers? Is the ethics of the officers' actions tied to the relative wrongdoing of the criminals?
2. Are laws the codification of the ethics of humanity at the time, or tied to a higher/universal law? There was a time when slavery was (*wrongly*) legal. Do citizens have an obligation to follow the law if it goes against their opinion of the ethics of the law passed?
3. If meat eating were made illegal by a duly elected government, would you continue to eat meat, or break the law? (*Assuming it caused no dietary issues to follow the law.*)
4. Are there individual rights that the government should not be allowed to take away, even if taking them away would benefit the common good? What are/are not some of those rights?
5. Addiction can be defined as the "psychological and physical inability to stop performing an action." By that definition, is the narrator addicted to meat? Should he try to give up his "addiction?" Are some addictions acceptable?

\* \* \*

# The Decay

## *Sierra Simopoulos*

\* \* \*

The waiting room had the familiar smell of too much hand sanitizer. Benjamin studied the cover of a curled magazine promising "30 New Positions to Heat Up Your Sex Life" before letting his attention wander to the secretary who incessantly beat her pen against the counter while staring at her papers.

"Soltz, Benjamin!"

He started at the sound of his name. Gripping his cane, he made his way up to the glass box.

"Mr. Soltz?" the woman asked without glancing up from her papers.

"That's right."

"Says here you need to refill a prescription?"

Benjamin nodded, fumbling to get the pill bottle from his pocket before finally placing it on the counter.

"Some morphine and whiskey is what I really need, but I guess this will do." He smiled weakly.

The woman didn't smile. She continued to stare at her

papers.

"It says here that you've reached your allotted drug limit for the month."

Benjamin looked up, confused. "That's never been an issue before."

"The government just passed a new bill that it will only cover the first hundred dollars for citizens over sixty-five. Don't you watch the news? Anyways, you'll have to pay for it if you want me to refill this."

Benjamin reached for his wallet. "How much will it be?"

"Seventy-two dollars, ten cents."

"Oh." He slowly returned his wallet to his pocket. "I guess maybe I'll just buy some of that whiskey instead." He tried to smile, but only managed to pull his lips into a tight line.

The woman finally looked up. "Maybe take a look at some of your options, Mr. Soltz? For your sake and that of your loved ones." She gave a practiced smile and slid a pamphlet across the counter. "Zhu, Alice!"

Benjamin stuffed the pamphlet into his pocket and left the clinic. He walked down the mall concourse toward the subway with careful, shuffling steps. Around him, screens flashed from store windows. A screen showing an image of two women with perfect faces laughing together told him *Our NEW SPRING LINE is here*. A lingerie ad displayed two people pressed against each other, emblazoned with the words, *Live while you're young*. As he got nearer, the faint light of the facial scanner flashed in his eyes. The lingerie ad blinked and changed to an ad for Kingsford Whiskey.

\* \* \*

Benjamin lowered himself onto his living room couch in

his small flat. His daughter Ania hated its ornate green and purple swirls, but he had picked it out with Felicity in their first year of marriage and he couldn't bring himself to throw it out.

He sat there for several minutes, watching the hand of the wall clock tick slow laps. He glanced at the TV remote, but the thought of cheery program hosts and never-ending advertisements felt overwhelming. Instead, he got up and made his way across the living room to the liquor cabinet. Moving aside empty bottles, he found one that had something left in it and poured the remainder into a glass on the end table. He lowered himself back onto the couch and took a sip. It was the kind of whiskey they sold at the convenience store, the kind that burned and smelled like burnt leather.

He looked at the picture of Ania that sat on the end table. She was grinning out from under a graduation cap. She looked happy here, happier than he had seen her in years. This had been the year before Felicity died. He remembered teaching Ania to climb the pear trees he and Felicity had planted in their backyard. He thought of the three of them hunting for worms together at Finn's Golf Course before their weekend fishing trips. A swelling pain rose in Benjamin's chest and his nose tickled unpleasantly. He chased the feeling away with another swig of whiskey.

His back began to throb from not taking his pain medication, and he reached instinctively into his jacket pocket for his pill bottle. Instead of the bottle, he found a crumpled piece of paper. He pulled it out, confused, and then remembered the pamphlet the woman at the clinic had given him. He smoothed it out.

*Let us help you transition from this life well.* The picture showed a young man and woman standing beside the bed of an elderly woman who looked like she was sleeping. The young people had big, perfect smiles.

He turned the pamphlet over. *You've lived an abundant life. Now it's time to pass the baton to the next generation. Our compassionate staff are here to make your last moments meaningful and comfortable. Medically-aided Cessation is a compassionate choice. Consider your options.*

Benjamin's hands shook as he stared at the pamphlet. Medically-aided Cessation. It was one of those topics that everyone thought about at some point when they were sitting alone and an ad for it popped up on TV, but of course it did not come up in polite conversation. Certainly, it was touched by conversation, "My aunt went to get put to rest this weekend" or "Toby's father is planning his going away party," but it was never talked about. Everyone knew people who had undergone the procedure. A few years before Benjamin had retired from Myers Construction, Francis, one of Benjamin's long-time coworkers, had not shown up for his Monday shift. It had been whispered, but never announced, that he had undergone the MAC procedure. He was a private man. He didn't like to make a big deal about these kinds of things. It was good that he should be at rest, after all. He had been a hardworking man, but now that his sight had been failing, what did he have left to live for? Continuing on would have been misery for him, the whispers had said.

*Consider your options.* His eyes lingered on these words.

At the bottom of the pamphlet, there was a phone number in large print. Benjamin glanced over to where his old telephone sat on the end table, covered in a layer of dust. He took another drink of whiskey.

Slowly, he reached for the receiver and dialed.

A cheerful woman's voice answered.

"Good afternoon. This is the National Institute of Life Care, Medically-Aided Cessation Branch. Could I get your name and citizen code?"

"Benjamin Soltz, 5N268FJ1."

"Are you calling to book an appointment?"

"I... well... I was just wondering... at what point in life do people usually make an appointment?"

"Well, it really varies from individual to individual. Most feel that when they can no longer live the life they want, it is the best option for them." There was a pause. "Are you considering the procedure?"

"I, uh..." Benjamin jammed the receiver back on its hook and stuffed the pamphlet into the coffee table drawer out of sight.

\* \* \*

Ania had given Benjamin a new watch a few months ago. She had shown him how to scroll on it to do all sorts of things: listen to music, use the calculator, look at pictures. He didn't remember how to do any of that now. He just wanted to make a phone call. Ania had said that she had saved her new phone number on the watch somewhere. He flipped through all the screens, squinting at the little glowing symbols, but didn't see anything that looked like a phone number. He scrolled through all the screens again and even tried clicking on one of the symbols, but it just opened another complex screen with some sort of graph on it. He exhaled heavily and got up from his kitchen table, piling his plate from breakfast on the others beside the sink.

He sank onto the couch and flipped the TV on. He didn't really watch, but it was good to be surrounded by the sound of other people's voices. Suddenly, his old telephone rang. *Ania.* He snapped off the TV and sent the remote skidding across the coffee table as he scrambled to grab the receiver.

"Hello?"

"Hello, is this Mr. Soltz?" Disappointment flooded Benjamin. It was a woman, but not Ania.

"Yes," he said. "Who's this?"

"Mr. Soltz, I'm calling from the National Institute of Life Care. We saw that you inquired about the MAC procedure, and I just wanted to see if you had any further questions about it."

Benjamin felt a pang of panic.

"N-no. No questions."

There was a brief pause. "Well, we are always here if you do."

"Well, j-just one question, actually..." Benjamin thought of Ania and felt his eyes grow wet. "Do people who get the procedure usually still have family?"

"Yes, quite often they do," the woman said. "Many feel that when they can no longer contribute to society or to their family this is the best option for them."

"What makes most people feel that they can no longer contribute?"

"Oh—well—there are different factors for different people. Being unable to contribute financially or posing difficulties of care on their loved ones. It's something everyone has to weigh for themselves."

"How do family members usually respond?"

"Well, many people decide not to tell their family members to prevent them from having to feel the guilt of agreeing with the decision. But others have family members who are supportive."

"I see. Thank you. G-goodbye."

"You have a good day, Mr. Soltz. Feel free to call if you have any further questions." There was a sharp click.

Benjamin stared at the receiver in his hand for a long time.

\* \* \*

The doctor said that Benjamin's morning walks were an important part of his overall health and wellness. Benjamin's lower back throbbed with every step and he leaned heavily on his cane. He'd gone through the bottle of subsidized painkillers before the end of the month again, even though he'd tried to spread out the dosage more than usual. As he made his way laboriously down the sidewalk, he was startled by a buzzing from his watch. He pressed repeatedly on the glowing screen.

"Ania? Ania?"

"Dad?" His daughter's voice sounded distorted.

"Dad, you're muting it. Stop pressing the screen. You only have to press it once. Listen, I'm going to stop by your place in twenty minutes."

"Sure, sweetheart." There was an electronic bloop and the call disconnected. "Ania? Damn thing!"

It had been months since he had seen her. His mood lifted and even his backache seemed to lessen.

He stopped at one of the fruit stands, where a lady he often bought from was resting under an umbrella. Ania had always loved pears.

"How are you, Helen?"

"Oh, you know, getting by. My little tyke just learned how to crawl. He's been making a real mess of the house."

"Oh? How old is he now?"

"Ten months. The little menace. He managed to pull all my baking supplies off the bottom shelf of the pantry yesterday. Spilled the cocoa powder everywhere!"

Benjamin cracked a small smile, peering over his thick spectacles at the fruit prices. He raised his eyebrows.

"Why are these so darned expensive?" he said, nodding to a tray of golden yellow pears.

"Ben, don't you give me a hard time." She shook a finger at him. "They're organic. And rare to find, mind you. Almost all the fruit these days comes from the vertical farms. But there are always those rich blighters who are asking for the organic stuff. It was a real pain to find a farmer willing to ship here."

"Are they any better?"

"Oh yeah. They're delicious—sweet and juicy to the core. I'd eat them all the time if it wouldn't break the bank."

"I'll take one. Do you mind wrapping it up for me? I don't want it to bruise. It's for my daughter."

Helen obliged, and Benjamin smiled as he tucked the pear in its brown-paper wrapping carefully into his jacket pocket.

\* \* \*

Benjamin moved around his flat as quickly as his rheumatism would allow, putting dishes in the sink and throwing a blanket over the couch to cover its old pattern. He opened the window, hoping the fresh air would make the place more appealing and hide the smell of stale whiskey. His watch suddenly vibrated again.

"Dad, I'm here."

He tried to press the watch face to respond when there was a knock on the door.

"Come on in," he called as his daughter pushed the door open.

"Why did you buy me this thing?" he asked, pressing on the watch in irritation.

Ania laughed. "You never used the phone I bought you. Besides, this is what everyone has now." She was wearing a small black dress that her mother would never have approved of and was carrying two bags of groceries.

"Well, come on in. Have a seat." She smiled as he gave her a one-armed hug around the groceries before seating himself on the couch. "How's the new job? Do you like being an immigration—whatcha call it?"

"An immigration case analyst. It's been really good."

"You know, I helped build the Kay Building just a block over from where you work. Can you see it from your office?"

"No, I'm on the west side."

"Oh. I was the project manager on that job, you know."

"Yeah," she gave a small smile, "you've mentioned it. Dad, I can't stay long, but I was in the area and I thought I should come by and make sure you were taking care of yourself and bring you some food." She set the bags of groceries on his kitchen floor and began unloading them into the fridge. Chicken, lettuce, tomatoes, a bag of pears. The pear in his pocket suddenly felt like a foolish gift. She had a good government job, while he was living off the pittance his pension gave him. She could buy herself organic pears whenever she wanted.

"I thought you were going to stay and talk awhile."

"Oh, Dad, you know I'd want to if I could. But some of my old university friends are in town, and I'm going to take them out."

"Oh, I was wondering why you were wearing that." He waved at her dress.

"Well, I can't let these good looks you and mom gave me go to waste." She flipped her long hair over her shoulder and flashed him a joking smile.

Her watch began to ring. "Dammit! Lane is calling. I gotta run, Dad." She kissed him on the cheek and headed for the door as she answered the ringing machine. "Lane, I'm so sorry! I'll be there in a few minutes. Just meet me in the parking—" Her voice was cut off as the door closed behind her.

A jolt of pain went through Benjamin at the sharp sound of the door clicking shut. He leaned against the back of the couch. For some reason, his heart was beating fast. There was a tight feeling in his chest, but his eyes were dry.

Abruptly, he got up and headed for the liquor cabinet. He shoved bottles to the side, digging right to the back corners, but all of them were empty. He cursed, knocking over bottles as he withdrew his shaking hands.

His mind flicked to the coffee table drawer. He'd kept the thought of its contents forcibly out of his mind, but it lingered constantly at the edge of his subconscious.

He slowly opened the drawer and pulled out the pamphlet. He read it again. Then, he dialed the big number.

"National Institute of Life Care, Medically-Aided Cessation Branch." It was a man's voice this time. "What is your name and citizen code?" Benjamin gave them.

"Our records show that you've called about an

appointment before?"

"I... yes. Yes, a little while ago. I was just wondering... about the procedure... how does it work?"

"Well, once you book a date, we'll have you come in to the clinic here. We'll go over any important last wishes and legal matters, so you'll want to make sure you bring any necessary documentation. We take care of all that with our in-clinic lawyers to make sure everything is as simple as possible for the client. Our staff will be here with you the whole time to make your last moments meaningful and comfortable. The procedure itself is straightforward and entirely painless." He paused. "Did you have any other questions about it?"

Benjamin didn't respond. A few months ago, he had decided to surprise Ania at her home. He had picked through all the flowers in the grocery store to find the best ones and even splurged on some wine with a fancy French label. Finding her place had been difficult. That side of the city had changed so much over the years and he had started to become nervous that the faded piece of paper with her address referred to a building that wasn't there anymore. But finally, he had found it, feeling rather pleased with himself. A man had opened the door, squinting and rubbing his eyes.

"What'd ya want, man?" His breath smelled of liquor.

"I was just stopping by to visit my daughter." Benjamin straightened up. The other man blinked at him stupidly.

"Ania? She's out."

"When will she be back?"

"She's a busy woman. Probably not until late tonight," said the man. Benjamin's shoulders slumped.

"Would you give her these for me?" He held out the

flowers and wine.

"Sure, man, sure." The man took them and closed the door. Benjamin had hoped Ania would call him when she got home and saw that he'd been there. But even though he stayed awake later than usual, he didn't hear from her.

"We have an availability this afternoon you could come in for."

"Oh... I... I was thinking maybe a few weeks from now?"

"It is of course your choice, but we highly recommend the procedure as soon as possible after the decision is made—it helps avoid any unnecessary stress or pain. Let me know what you prefer."

There was a long pause.

"Are you still there, Mr. Soltz?"

Benjamin remembered Ania at six or seven, smiling down at him proudly from where she had climbed up on the roof by scaling one of the trees in the backyard. Felicity had been nearly hysterical, but Benjamin had laughed, calling her his little squirrel. She had been so pleased with herself until she tried to climb back down. Suddenly, she burst into tears, kicking her legs as she held onto the roof and struggled for purchase with her feet. Benjamin had been up the tree in an instant, catching her legs and drawing her to the trunk.

Tears began to roll down his cheeks. He thought of her as she had been this afternoon, rushing out to meet people he had never heard of. She had moved on from the back garden to a world of glass office buildings, a world where she didn't need him.

"Mr. Soltz? I can book you in for six o'clock if you'd like."

"Six o'clock would be fine."

\* \* \*

Benjamin had to take the subway all the way downtown to get to the clinic. Every time the subway stopped he gripped his cane shakily with both hands. A woman got up from her seat a short way down the car. Benjamin shuffled carefully in that direction. A teen blaring music through his headphones slid into the seat.

\* \* \*

The glass doors moved smoothly to the side as Benjamin entered the clinic. A bright-eyed woman who stood just inside directed him to the palm scanner. The blue light under his hand flashed and the woman checked her tablet.

"Ah yes. I see you have an appointment for 6:00, Mr. Soltz?" Benjamin nodded. "Right this way, please."

She led him to a room with a large, four-poster bed, a small wooden desk, and a manicured tree in the corner.

"If you will just wait here, Doctors Emerson and Schneider will be with you shortly. Feel free to make yourself comfortable."

Benjamin sat on the edge of the bed. It smelled vaguely of lavender.

The door opened and a man and woman entered.

"Mr. Soltz? Pleased to meet you," said the man, smiling and extending his hand. It was warm and firm. "I'm Dr. Emerson and this is my colleague, Dr. Schneider." A woman with very red fingernails took his hand. "We are here to discuss your transition from this life," continued the man. "First of all, do you have any questions for us?"

"Um. I—I want to tell my daughter. But I don't know how."

"Mr. Soltz," said the woman, "sometimes the best thing we can do for someone we love is to free them from the weight of having to choose. Many people's family members feel the obligation to try to dissuade someone from making this choice, even if they know it's best. We recommend, though this is of course your choice, that you make this decision on your own so that your daughter doesn't have to carry the weight of worrying that she made the wrong decision after you're gone."

Ania would try to stop him. Benjamin knew it. His heart lightened at the thought. But it quickly plummeted again. She'd put him in some expensive home, and he'd be even more of a burden on her.

"Many patients write a letter," the woman suggested, "for after they are gone."

Benjamin nodded.

"Yes, I'd like that."

The woman took out a stack of thick paper and a pen. "We know this can be an emotional time, so we'll leave you alone to have some time to write. Just press the button on the wall when you are finished." She set the materials on the desk, and the two doctors left the room.

Benjamin picked up the pen and started to write in his slow, careful hand.

\* \* \*

*Dear Ania,*

He paused, trying to process what he could say.

*I'm sorry I didn't tell you about this decision before it happened. I didn't want it to weigh on you. I know you would have taken care of me, but I didn't want to be a burden to you. I don't want you to feel bad now. I want you to live your life to the fullest. I'm going to have them leave you everything. It's not much, but with the money from the flat hopefully you can buy your own place and be more secure than your mother and I were when we started out. I love you so much and I'm so proud of you.*

*All my love,*
*Dad*

\* \* \*

He read it again and his eyes teared up in frustration. It felt flat and inadequate. It didn't say all the things he felt at all. But he didn't know how to say it any better. He set it down on the desk before pushing the button on the wall.

The male doctor re-emerged almost instantly with another man who he introduced as the in-clinic lawyer.

The legal proceedings were quite quick. Benjamin told him everything was to go to Ania and signed the places he needed to. Benjamin was then left alone again for a few minutes and moved back to the bed, shifting around as he sat on the edge. Finally, the male and female doctor came back.

"Everything seems to be in order," said the man. "Now, we also want to thank you for considering the future of our nation with this decision, Mr. Soltz. It's important that all citizens think about how their lives fit into the rest of society. With limited funding for medical care, this decision could allow a young child to have the resources to have the lifesaving operation that they need. You are a hero, Mr. Soltz. As a gesture of our gratitude for your decision, the government will cover all the expenses for this procedure and the funeral and will also plant a tree in your name."

"Would you like to choose your tree, Mr. Soltz?" asked the woman, holding out a brochure.

Benjamin looked up. "Maybe a pear tree?"

The woman's smile faltered for a split second. "I'm sorry, Mr. Soltz. That isn't one of the options that we have on hand. How about we plant a nice poplar for you?" She pointed at the glossy picture with one of her red nails.

"Oh… That would be alright."

"Mr. Soltz, I'm going to ask you to lie back here on the bed and relax," said the man, pressing gently on Benjamin's shoulder. The bed was overwhelmingly soft. The duvet was going to swallow him. Panic began to rise. He would never see Ania again.

"You are doing the right thing." The woman looked down at him with that perfect smile. "This will help you relax." She covered his nose and mouth with a mask. His vision blurred.

He had to see Ania again. He had to hug her one last time.

He felt a sharp prick in his arm. A moment of terror filled him. It died away quickly.

\* \* \*

The mortician unzipped the bag to remove personal effects and clothing from the body before cremation. He placed the wallet and keys in a demarcated container. While removing the man's jacket, he noticed a strange lump in the coat pocket and pulled out a bruised pear wrapped in brown paper. He dropped it into the trash bin.

\* \* \*

*This story first appeared in the After Dinner Conversation—April 2022 issue.*

## Discussion Questions

1. The woman on the phone tells Benjamin that people choose to die when "they can no longer live the life they want" or because they are a burden to their family, or unable to contribute financially. Do you think any of these are good enough reasons to choose to die?
2. What, if any, is a good enough reason to choose to die? Do people have a moral obligation to stay alive as long as possible?
3. Should Benjamin have told his daughter what he was going to do before he died, or did he make the right decision in sparing her the guilt of trying to talk her out of stopping him?
4. If you were able to talk to Benjamin, what would you have advised him to do?
5. What is the societal purpose for someone like Benjamin? Are people required to have a valuable societal purpose to justify their use of limited resources?

* * *

# The Kill Registry

*Brian Howlett*

\* \* \*

My sister chose to use her bullet years ago and ever since she has badgered me to liberate my own from its chamber. Beth leveled her pistol at her husband five years into their marriage, and she has no regrets, which is one of the things I admire about her. I was the first person she called after the smoke cleared. By the time I arrived, she was watching TV, waiting for the Ministry of Mortality to come and retrieve the body. "It's on the balcony," she said helpfully. I didn't need to look, so I joined her in the living room and changed the channel as if it were any other visit. "People are right," she continued. "It was the best decision I could have made. There is no point in waiting for old age and then, what, take my bullet into the grave?" She said this last part accusingly.

But I don't have any one person in my life who stands between me and happiness, like some traffic cop with their arm raised. I'm not married. I love my job. Have great friends. However, I am threatening to hit thirty years old, so I am also aware of the danger of turning into one of our aunts and uncles, who gather around their generous pours of red, white, and beer, pining over the fact that they've never taken their allotted kill, and that it's too late for them.

"If I had only taken out Professor Willoughby, then I would have graduated with a better mark and found a better law firm to intern with." Uncle Archie. "If I had killed Coach Clemons, then I would have been showcased properly for the scholarships to the good schools." Aunt Jerry. These are the toothless observations of things long passed. *If* is a word for the weak and the broken-hearted.

Beth executed an all-too-common kill; spouse on spouse. Paolo wasn't cheating on her. He didn't drink or smoke weed. He didn't golf or gamble or even watch sports. He gave the rest of us nothing to talk about. And that was his greatest sin, at least in Beth's mind. I suspect that he may still be standing if he had suffered from a few interesting vices. As she went on to explain, she had no choice.

"Tuesday is my worst day of the week, as you know," she began.

I turned the volume down on the TV. It was the least I could do out of respect for Paolo.

"I came into the kitchen and there he was, sipping weakly at his morning coffee as if the poor soul was afraid of the hot liquid itself. Or the mug, with its cracked handle. Jesus, he was afraid of the sunrise. The neighbors down the hall who are too loud some nights. The traffic on the way to work. The boss who is waiting for him."

The boss would be waiting for a while.

Beth sipped at her Yeti container of tea. Tiny,

apprehensive sips. I kept quiet. "Poor Paolo," she finally said quietly. Surely, a part of her would miss a part of him?

"Even the squirrels in the trees," she continued, shaking her head. "The man was frightened of everything. Me, most of all."

This was news to me, but maybe she was already engaging in revisionist history. Maybe what happened is that Beth suddenly saw what so many others had already seen; simply that she was married to a boring man. The only interesting thing about him was his name, at least where we come from, which is a neighborhood filled with Dans and Ricks and Jims.

Paolo was set to remain attached to Beth's hip until they withered into arthritic old age. Dying together in front of the Local News at Six. Paolo didn't possess the imagination it might take to divorce Beth. And she didn't want to deal with the financial fallout if she initiated it, seeing as how she earned triple what he did.

I would have raised the alarm bells if Beth had thought to ask my opinion of him when they announced their engagement, but I was forced to play the part of the dutiful best friend and brother and watch her amble down the aisle to what I knew to be certain disappointment. We danced that night at the parish hall; uncles and aunts, cousins, adolescents sneaking drinks, priests drinking in the open, and of course, those of us in the wedding party, who on that day, were aglow with our proximity to the holy couple, but still being single, were blessed with the taint of something sexual rather than marital. On Beth's second dance as a married woman, she came close to me on the dance floor, and every spin and turn was an opportunity for me to come whisper into my best friend's ear, "It's not too late."

But I didn't. And she twirled away from me, her face reflecting the vivid, cheap fluorescent lights from above, a woman happy in a golden moment. I knew that this marriage to an overmatched mate didn't have to be a tragedy. She possessed the kill shot.

She finished by telling me that the revelation had taken her by surprise, like a window slamming shut on itself. With one stir of the honey into the Yeti, she decided that she would assign her one legal kill, shoot her dear witless husband, and make herself a free woman.

It was a clean kill. The event didn't raise eyebrows. Sanctioned kills never do. Husbands kill wives. Sisters kill brothers. Workers kill bosses.

Who would be my mark? I often fantasize about this. On my way to work, maybe it's the guy who butts in front of me to get onto the crowded subway and who then takes up two seats. Or the woman at the medical center who tells me, after I've waited two long hours, that there is a glitch in the booking system, and that I will have to come back another day for an appointment. It might be the idiot who swerves in front of me as I'm merging onto the freeway. The food delivery guy who brings my pizza to the door late and stone cold and still expects me to tip him. *I'll tip you, all right.*

I will take out my government-approved pistol that is designed to be 95 percent accurate within ten feet and calmly shoot him. Shoot them all. They will protest, but not too much. Or they will run, but they won't get away. As we have all been instructed, they will know that their time is up. That they have crossed the wrong person. The wrong lover or stranger. Their name is about to be entered into The Registry.

But I resist the temptation. My pistol has remained holstered since I received my license. We are blessed with just one bullet at birth and are taught from an early age about the values of patience and prudence.

The streetcar stopped in front of my factory in the west end. A cyclist didn't stop when I stepped from it and she almost ran me over. *Bang bang, you're dead.*

I work in the city's manufacturing hub, along the railway tracks that most people don't realize still work their way through our metropolitan core. Trains running at night don't make a sound in the big city.

My company makes athletic footwear. Turn on the TV; the guy making the big dunk has gained a quarter inch of air thanks to a patented composite material in the sole of his shoe that my team developed. The wide receiver responsible for the weekly highlight reel catch on the sidelines runs a tighter route because his cleats are several ounces lighter, a result of a three-year project spearheaded by my colleague and work spouse, Ally.

Ally and I started with Aspar Atletica at the same time. She joined from a prestigious design school, while I arrived via a more circuitous route: gaining experience on the shop floor while going to a community college and managing to win a national industrial design competition for an entirely recyclable shoe prototype.

We share everything at work, including our confusion over the missing "h" and extra "a" in "Atletica," even though the affectation does appeal to our creative sensibilities. We can both admit, at least to each other, that we're design whores. Aspar is a company of five hundred, and Ally and I are the only creatives apart from a few interns, so we need to defend our role within the corporate culture by amplifying it. Two against the world. So, when she invited me to lunch, I didn't hesitate. Maybe there was a new product in the pipeline on the football side of things, which could augur well for the basketball division.

I arrived at the bistro to see that she had ordered us both a beer. This was strange, as she knows I don't like to drink during the day.

"I hope you don't mind," she said, speaking a little too quickly, as I also tend to do in her presence. I tried not to look at her legs under the table as I took my seat. When we first met, I wanted to ask her out, and I suspected that she would accept. But I wasn't ready for someone like her. It would be too real, so I put my feelings away, as if in a shoebox. But whenever we are alone, sitting close like this, the lid comes off.

She raised her glass.

"What are we celebrating?"

"Don't worry, I'm not engaged."

What a bitch. "Why would I be worried?"

She had been living with Jerome for several years. And maybe if she did get engaged, it wouldn't be so awful. It would put her in the shoebox for good. Being smarter than me, she knew exactly how I felt about her, even if I had never articulated it.

"But it is a merger. Beeball. Football. Together at last."

"What?"

"Our two divisions are coming closer together." I suspect she would have brought her hands together and interlaced her fingers to demonstrate the act if she wasn't so clearly enjoying caressing the sides of the cold beer glass.

"That makes no sense. And how did you find out?"

*Before me,* I didn't need to add.

The shine came off her smile, and she attempted to hide behind the rim of the glass.

"Basketball and football; it's completely different engineering," I persisted, explaining it to myself more than to her. "Two different worlds. Hardwood and controlled climate versus turf, grass, snow, and rain. We don't even source materials from the same places."

"Wrong. They are made from the same materials. Money."

My glass remained on the table.

"They've been talking cost cutting forever, you know that. And so, here we are," she continued. "Don't do that thing."

"What thing?"

"That looking off into space thing that you do. Your *I'm tuning you and the whole world out* expression, that glazed look. It isn't attractive. As if you don't want to hear about sales and numbers. That you're somehow above that. Bullshit. You're as horny for the sales bonuses as I am."

"Well, it's not what we studied in school, is it? I thought it was all about design innovation. Besides, I haven't seen anyone lower the price of our shoes, have you? Last I saw, the Seven V High-Top retails for two-forty-nine and two-seventy-nine just in time for back to school. Surely our German owners are capable of slicing a nice bit of profit out of that cake."

"They just want a bigger slice. Which is what they've asked me to do."

"Oh."

"Don't do that, either," she continued. "Say 'oh' like that.

Listen, it's not like I'll ever be your boss."

"Except it sounds like you'll be my boss."

"We'll always be equal partners in this."

I'm not stupid enough to trust what even a good friend says. We're born as one, we live as one, and we die as one. Good friends are fractionally more trustworthy than strangers when it comes to self-interest. I had seen enough hushed meetings in the Aspar boardroom among the senior leadership group to know that multiple discussions concern me but don't involve me. And now, Ally will be at that table. Worse, she belongs there. She will be great, and we both know it.

"And if you think lunch is on me, you're mistaken," she said, smiling, trying to get back on solid ground.

"Speaking of design," I said, leaving the refrain unspoken. I unholstered my pistol and set it on the table.

It had just arrived by registered mail. She picked up the gleaming weapon. It was more black than silver but reflected the glints of sunlight coming in through the window as she turned it over in her hand.

"You're not supposed to do that. It's in my name." I looked around the bar, but she simply laughed. Delighted.

"Wow. You're so lucky. I haven't seen the latest. It's much lighter than I thought. Slimmer, too. Impressive."

"Just like shoes. Continuous improvement. Sometimes even the government gets it right."

The federal government redesigns the gun every five years. The goal is to make the strike even more accurate. In the early days, there were too many messy cleanups required. The Ministry wants the kills to be clean. There is no second bullet allowed, so if you miss, it creates complications.

"You have to put that away, miss." The waitress was at our table with two very large menus listing things that entire swaths of their customer base will never eat. She gestured to the large sign behind the bar that many establishments display: *This bar and restaurant is a No-Kill zone.* Individual commercial enterprises lobbied for the right to institute their policy several years after The Kill Registry passed into law. Aspar allowed us to bring our guns to work. In this, they are typical of most large companies. Many public spaces, including arenas and even some churches, didn't oppose it either. But there is a growing number of dining establishments beginning to say, "No, you can't carry out your kill here. We have spent far too much time and money on creating appetite appeal for you to splay guts against the wall, as accurate as the shot may be."

Embarrassed by the waitress, I took the gun from Ally's hands. It had been several years since I had touched her fingers.

"Would you kill me if I told you I was marrying Jerome?"

"No." And that was the truth.

"That's too bad," she replied. "And I don't think he would kill me if I was to marry you. Poor me."

When Ally showed up at Aspar two weeks after I started with the company, I immediately looked her up on The Kill Registry, as you do upon meeting someone new. The brief write-up stated that she was twenty at the time and still at university. Far too young. Use your bullet so early in life, and it closes too many doors. How can you possibly know at such a young age that the person you've chosen to silence is the one? But of course, it doesn't seem to have slowed her down any, and today, maybe because of that, everything she does seems more measured than anyone else at Aspar. You would never guess that at one point in her life, she was prone to giving in to the moment.

Economists have Milton Keynes. Sociologists have Mia Baumann, a Geneva-based criminologist who argued in her doctoral thesis that the mortality rate would be reduced by 18 percent if everyone is permitted to kill one person without consequence. Dr. Baumann proposed that it would make people think twice before committing the act: if you know that you can kill someone with impunity, then you will wait for just the right occasion. If you are in a hostile situation in which one might normally pull the trigger in a fit of passion, you will pause and ask yourself if this is the person you want to use your one bullet on. A kill becomes an asset; something you save up like money for a rainy day. And as the statistics laid out, many people die without touching their rainy-day funds.

Her paper, "A Proposed New Role and Strategy of Government in Terms of Fighting the Epidemic of Violence Across Socio Economic Strata," once published, caused a stir in academia, but would otherwise have disappeared into the academic void along with so many other groundbreaking ideas if not for the campaign of a politician from Louisiana, who, throwing a Hail Mary on a losing senatorial race, mentioned Baumann's idea in her speech. It spread like wildfire with the outraged critics huffing and puffing and fanning the flames. By the end of the campaign cycle, the concept had gained national attention and informed the governor's platform and was passed into law several years later. In one of the great ironies of the age, a rival professor from Harvard who vehemently challenged the thesis because it was sheer lunacy, finally had enough and, years later, boarded a plane to Geneva where he showed up in

Baumann's lecture hall, promptly approached the lectern and raised his government-issued gun. He later said that it went off by accident. Legend has it that the last thing Baumann said, looking the intruding professor in the eye, was "So, you do agree with me after all."

No one ever circled back to see if the 18 percent reduction forecast by the professor was ever borne out. The math didn't matter. Being able to kill one person was too attractive on a universal level for it to ever be challenged. The Kill Registry became as fundamental to society as was freedom of speech. At the age of eighteen, you were invited to a half-day seminar teaching you how to aim and fire to ensure success. Upon certification, you were given your gun. It was a special one-bullet chamber, and it came loaded.

"But you," I said to Ally. "You did choose love." The waitress came over again, but I waved her off. Seeing her made my blood rise a tick higher. Again, I fantasized about eliminating the minor annoyances in my day. But if I did kill the waitress the restaurant would just replace her with someone equally pestering.

"We can't take too long, Geoff. We have to get back."

"I'm guessing that this is my new boss talking?"

"If that's how you need to put it."

Unlike Paolo, Ally's boyfriend in her second year at school did entertain a vice. Ally shot him in the back, which was naked at the time as he was on top of her roommate. She didn't hesitate. Was it a moment she would like to take back? Did she wish that she would have been blessed with a second bullet, so that she could kill her roommate too? I've never asked.

"I don't think I want lunch," I said, pushing the menu

away. I got up. "But go ahead, finish your beer. I'll see you back there."

"This is ridiculous. I'll head back with you. I can grab takeout."

I went straight to the exit, and she followed. "The appointment isn't official for another two weeks, so we can talk about this some more after you've had some time to think about it." She had caught up to me in the parking lot. "I can tell you more about how the new organization is going to be structured."

I was eager to get back to the privacy of my office.

"Don't worry. Your job isn't going to change."

Was I now obligated to listen to her? Could I no longer just tell her to go to hell and return to my work?

"Where will you be sitting now?"

"Don't be stupid; the same place as always. It's not that big a deal."

I wished that she would stop lying and turn to me and say, *This is an amazing promotion. I'm getting a bunch more money, and now I'm going to be able to kick you and the entire basketball division in the ass whenever I want.* I wanted her to jump up and down and hug me and say, *I can't wait!*

I turned to her. It was me who took her by the shoulders.

"I get it," I started. "A job is everything. Especially for the lucky ones like you and me."

She wasn't following, but this was something that I often thought about.

"We have the best jobs in the world."

"I guess, sure." If she hadn't reddened when announcing her promotion, she certainly did now.

"Like I said. You chose love when you were a kid. But if

that asshole boyfriend of yours never cheated, and you were still sitting on your one bullet today, you may never have to use it. You've got it all."

"Thanks. That's sweet. Honestly, this promotion is going to be good for both of us. We'll finally have a voice with the senior leadership group. Give me time, and I'll ask for more money for product innovation. It won't be just about cutting costs anymore."

I didn't look convinced.

"Don't you see, we'll be at the table."

If I had asked her out when we met, what then? Would she have moved in with me rather than Jerome? Would one of us then have moved on from Aspar to comply with company policy? There are only so many jobs in industrial shoe design, so that would prove another obstacle.

I never imagined that it would be like this. I redrew my gun.

"Right," she said, almost laughing. She turned to go.

But I held firm and raised the gun. I didn't have much time. The law is clear on this; the victim has every right to oppose the action. I didn't want Ally running. I might miss a moving target. It had been years since I shot the placebo gun at the seminar. Besides, what if some of her professional football clients had taught her a few moves? She could run straight and then, just as I fired, cut right. A down and out.

The smile left her face as I stepped closer. She looked confused. I could only hope that she saw some kindness in my eyes, but more so, that she understood I was picking work over love. The trigger action was surprisingly smooth, and she fell gently to the sidewalk.

I entered my registration number in The Kill Registry app. The Ministry would be here shortly, so I could leave. I had a meeting to attend.

* * *

*This story first appeared in the After Dinner Conversation—December 2022 issue.*

## Discussion Questions

1. Why did the narrator kill Ally? Was it for work, for love, or for some other reason?
2. If you had one free kill, would you have already used it? If so, who/when would you have used it? What would have changed in your life by using it?
3. If you knew you could be legally killed at any time, how would you live your life differently? How would your interactions with others be different? Is there anyone you think would have already killed you?
4. If people were allowed one free kill, do you think it would typically be used rationally or in a fit of passion? What is your reasoning?
5. Would you support this law, or some variation of this law, being passed in real life?

* * *

# The Crate

## David Rich

\* \* \*

I cruised out of BLE's house in my crate. A teenaged girl like myself, she was one of the few people I'd ever seen in person.

I stopped my crate in no place in particular to flat out break the law. I was so good at hacking crates that I'd reprogrammed mine to open upon command. Crazy illegal!

All crates were programmed to protect everyone's fundamental right not to be seen. Basically, they remained closed until confirming you're in the presence of only legally sanctioned live contacts. Then you go back in before seeing any unauthorized people.

History recounts that long ago, people judged one another by things such as gender, ethnicity, occupation, personal transportation vehicle, etc. But the modern American Political Union, our beloved A.P.U., made that intrinsically impossible.

When the door opened, I stepped out of my crate into

broad daylight. Although my actions were illicit, I expected no witnesses and deemed them as harmless.

I viewed a sea of crates, perfectly identical boxes on wheels, rolling to their individual destinations. Inside each, I imagined a human being enjoying physical isolation by texting, gaming, taking in media, or any number of things.

Then, I glimpsed a mother and child crossing the street. I believe they were of Asian descent (though we rarely spoke of ethnic physical traits). Certainly, they'd legally arranged to walk wherever they were headed. But we weren't supposed to see one another.

The girl stared at me; she didn't appear old enough to understand the law. When the mother spotted me, she made her daughter look away and hurried her along.

The moment was amazing. They were two random people I'd never seen before. Above all, I'd beaten the system. I was powerful. The mother who'd seen me couldn't disguise her horror.

It was exhilarating.

\* \* \*

Of the people I'd known in person, all but BLE were family relations. BLE was my only "live" friend; all my remaining friends were still virtual. It was a sore subject for me. I suspect that by my age, most had several legally sanctioned live friends.

I remembered hacking BLE's crate profile and learning that she had six live friends and many more virtual friends than I did. Knowing things like that was forbidden because comparisons can make people feel inferior. And in this case, I was angry! It'd made no sense to me that she'd have more friends.

I knew I was much smarter than BLE and made frequent hints about it without telling her explicitly. I couldn't risk that she'd lodge a complaint, or worse, record the conversation.

If you denigrated anyone, they caught you. If you compared and contrasted people's merits and flaws, they caught you.

I'd been accused of revealing my own accomplishments from time to time. Usually, the AI's caught it in my text messages. Fortunately, minor correct speech violations resulted in either warnings or assignments to watch dreadful reeducation videos.

One had to be subtle. So, earlier that afternoon, I'd managed a casual comment regarding the ease of last week's chemistry exam. Her riled glance was priceless.

Despite our complicated relationship, we were indispensable allies in solving a mutual problem.

We both wanted to flee the American Political Union.

It seemed obvious why I'd want to leave. How infuriating it had been, possessing superior intelligence, to be considered merely an equal in a sea of perfectly identical crates!

But BLE?

I knew she was distinctively pleasant and engaging in person, though I had minimal data to compare. Perhaps I'd always suspected she didn't belong hidden in a crate.

*The hare came through*, BLE texted. In our secret code, that meant one of her many friendship connections had provided the geographic coordinates of a gap in the electronic border fence confining the A.P.U.'s population.

*About a thousand rabbit holes*, she continued texting. That meant the ride to the gap was a thousand kilometers. A long way! But I'd successfully mastered how to disable our crates' travel limiters and location transmitters without losing auto-navigation. The next steps simply were to choose a day and cover story, empty our currency accounts, and set the coordinates.

I didn't suspect a crate would fit through the border hole. However, according to BLE, it was only a ten kilometer walk across the neutral zone to a border checkpoint of the O.A.R., the Old American Republic.

It was common knowledge that the O.A.R. accepted defectors from the American Political Union, honoring the two nations' shared history. More importantly, the O.A.R. appreciated the A.P.U.'s strong educational system. With my advanced ability, I anticipated many advantages for myself in the O.A.R.

However, I couldn't foresee as much for BLE.

\* \* \*

Finally, our day of flight came. My plan was so perfect, it was anticlimactic. Our parents never questioned our lie that we were visiting one another. My ingenuity with the crates' innards worked flawlessly. So, I spent most of our transit reading an old novel written before the Second American Civil War.

When we arrived at the gap, we stepped out of our crates into the open sun. We slid right through the border gap.

The hike across the neutral zone was magnificent. Having seen drone videos of A.P.U. Protected Forests hadn't prepared me for the experience of physically walking through nature.

I felt lightheaded upon approaching the Old American Republic border checkpoint. An armed man led us to a waiting area. Quaint paper FAQs indicated that our petitions for defection would be reviewed upon testing and evaluation.

Another man escorted me to a room where I received a multi-subject written exam. The proctor observed me carefully and took notes. Perhaps he was wary of cheaters. But I didn't need to cheat. I crushed the test despite the proctor's irritating stare. Clearly, the O.A.R. badly needed bright people like me!

I paced alone for what seemed like hours. For the first time, my triumph wouldn't remain secret. Soon, I'd have the opportunity to pursue the great life I deserved.

Then, a smiley gentleman entered. From his uniform, I presumed he was important.

"Ma'am, I'm Dan Brendan, O.A.R. Immigration Agent. You'll be pleased with the results of your exam."

I recognized his accent, relaxed and slow, but had never heard it from a live individual. Nevertheless, I savored the praise, eager for more.

"Congratulations JNA-9468," continued Brendan as my anticipation swelled. "Your O.A.R. citizenship application has been hereby granted. Welcome to the land of the free."

I eagerly anticipated my future success in a world where people could be openly compared!

He resumed, "Your being so smart, I reckon you'll want to attend one of our universities. But first we need to discuss your categorization results. You'll belong to Category D, I'm afraid."

That didn't sound too awful. "So...?"

"At school, you'll reside in a Category D living group. If your high achievement continues, you'll have opportunities to work at numerous corporations. But frankly, there'll be limits to what positions you're eligible to hold, what neighborhoods you can live in, who you can marry, and numerous other things."

"I don't understand. Is this because I wasn't born here?"

"That often affects the decision, but not here. Look, our great Old American Republic has four levels: A, B, C, and D."

"And D is the *lowest*? What was my test score? I killed it!"

"The fact you've been admitted here means you did sufficiently well... given your, umm, circumstances."

"What circumstances?"

"You don't know, do you? You and your ridiculous crates. No one's ever told you, have they?"

My stomach fluttered and gurgled. "What?"

"Ma'am, here in the Old American Republic, you're... well... ugly as a dog!" He laughed. "And quite overweight."

"Do you know how *offensive* that is?!"

I couldn't believe my ears. His language went far beyond anything I'd ever heard. In the A.P.U., he'd have suffered more than reeducation videos! In fact, I'm fairly certain he could've been incarcerated under the Correct Speech Act of 2071.

But this wasn't the A.P.U.; it was the O.A.R.

"You seem irate. But expect others to put it less gently."

I was almost missing my crate. BLE and I quickly needed a change of plans!

"Where's my friend BLE? We need to talk."

"BLE-2384? Her new name's 'Bella.' Her exam just missed the margin, but we gave her an extra bump. She's Category B and headed to her new residence."

"What? How did she—"

"You have no sense of reference, do you? Bella's hot! A piece of ass!"

I'd never heard the expression "piece of ass." I let it go.

"If she's so wonderful, why isn't she Category A?"

"Category A? That's for men only! But don't worry about Bella, that sweet thing'll become a pharmaceutical sales rep or news commentator... or anywhere we need a woman in the meeting room to gawk at. Heck, maybe she'll be your boss one day."

I couldn't imagine what vile mode of thinking created a place like this. I was able to run circles around BLE.

Gravely regretting having fled the A.P.U., I was stuck and needed to adjust. Borrowing from *JNA-9468*, I became Janet Niner.

To my delight, several colleges accepted me. Though the odds were stacked against me, I had choices. I traveled across beautiful country to the university I'd selected. My advanced level allowed me to enroll as a sophomore. The Category D living arrangements were cramped, but not as bad as I'd feared.

My roommate Alex was awesome. Her mother had taught her to retain a positive attitude in tough circumstances. I'd known that the A.P.U. had a diverse population, but since everyone hid in crates, it felt entirely theoretical. Although I'd been taught the importance of racial equality, Alex was the first person of African heritage I'd met in person. The more I got to know her, the more I appreciated being free of my crate.

Langer and Jason lived across the hall. According to Alex, they were lovers.

Regretfully, my first glance at Langer was sideways with my brows lowered and nose raised. He must have seen similar looks often, as homosexuality in the O.A.R. had an awful stigma.

I, however, had grown up in the A.P.U., where sexual

orientation was like eye color, all shades thoroughly normal. I was the one perfectly comfortable with it!

There were entirely other reasons, I admit shamefully, for not taking well at first to Langer. Since arriving in the O.A.R., having seen multitudes of live people, I'd begun building comparative yardsticks and found myself brazenly judging others as human instincts dictated.

Langer was tall, but skin and bones. His top jaw jutted forward hideously. His unpleasant face and lack of muscle tone made me uneasy. My glance of disgust must have caused hurt.

His roommate Jason was comically tiny next to Langer. At first, I couldn't take seriously anything puny Jason had to say.

I recognized that my prejudices clashed with my upbringing. But now surrounded by real people, nature was taking over.

Two weeks into school, I'd gotten used to the nasty looks from the Category B's and C's. The university's few A's lived in a Greek-lettered fraternity house. All of them were tall, sturdy, handsome men from select European heritage.

Being a D was tough. We were freely mocked and rarely shown any respect. Every day, someone demeaned me in some manner.

Near the end of my first semester, Langer was in a tough scrape. Another student, a C to my best guess, was punching him around. I assumed this "miscreant" disliked Langer for his sexual orientation. Regardless, Langer was on the ground about to be pummeled. A crowd had gathered to watch.

I don't know what made me do this, but I couldn't let him beat on my fellow D. I leapt out of the crowd and shoved Miscreant with the power of spontaneous rage. He stumbled two meters and tumbled to the ground.

I suddenly realized that I'd been a fool with a death wish for having done that. So, I disappeared among the onlookers before Miscreant could stand up. He never saw me. The crowd could have given me up, my being a D. Fortunately, they didn't seem to care.

Langer successfully escaped. However, my luck appeared to evaporate when a man in a military uniform intercepted me as I fled. He grabbed my arm, though not forcefully. I was terrified of the punishment I'd receive for violence committed against a person of higher category level.

"Janet Niner," he said.

"Please forgive me," I begged contritely, having no idea how he knew my name.

"Are you Janet Niner?"

"Yes sir."

"Someone important needs to speak with you... And your apology baffles me."

Apparently, he was ignorant of my attack upon Miscreant and couldn't have cared less.

\* \* \*

An hour later, I sat in an office in a building reserved for deans and faculty. The man across the desk from me wore a military uniform suggesting significant seniority. In addition to his decorations and rank insignia, he sported a gold pin with the Greek letters of the category A fraternity.

"Please address me as Colonel Hayden," he said. "And frankly, Janet, we need your help."

"*My* help?"

"Everything I'm about to tell you is confidential and

need-to-know. More to the point, if you violate this confidentiality, you'll wind up in a casket."

He had a direct way of speaking. I pondered my chances of surviving the day should I have refused to help him.

He continued, "I understand you have personal experience with crates."

"I'm from the A.P.U.; everyone uses crates."

"No. Specific expertise in electromechanical tampering and code manipulation."

Wondering how he knew that, I imagined lying pointless. I replied with a stutter, "Yes sir... Colonel Hayden."

"I also understand you're one of the more gifted students in the Electrical Engineering Department."

When I'd lived in the A.P.U., I'd ached to hear that type of praise. But after all I'd been through, the comment made me barely crack a smile.

Hayden continued, "We've acquired some crates and require your help. We need you to reprogram them to deliver packages to several highly secure and sensitive geographic coordinates in the A.P.U. You'll need to evade all security protocols designed to protect those locations."

The challenge sounded close to impossible, but I was confident I could ultimately succeed with enough time and additional intelligence regarding the electronic border fence. However, I didn't like the sound of it. It smelled of assassination or terrorism.

"What type of packages?"

Hayden sighed. "Nonlethal electromagnetic impulse weapons designed to disable heavily shielded electronics."

"What are the targets?"

He sighed again. "You have a lot of questions, don't you? It's need-to-know."

"To reprogram the crates, won't I need to know?"

"Are you committing to helping us?"

I lowered my head. I had no idea what I was getting into or what consequences my actions would bring.

"If you demonstrate your patriotism by helping us," Hayden said in a discreet and softer tone, "I can elevate your category level to C. Perhaps even B."

At that moment I should have felt elated. It was the opportunity for things to finally go my way. I was being recognized for my intellectual skills, and my efforts would elevate my social rank. These were the very things I'd hungered for from the beginning when I'd defected from the A.P.U. with BLE. I should have leapt out of my seat and thanked him!

But instead, I sat still, unable to look him in the eye. After all I'd been through, his offer didn't feel comfortable.

"And to answer your question," Hayden said, "the targets are the information systems governing the A.P.U.'s Right-Not-to-Be-Seen database and algorithms. Taken down, two hundred million crates will have no information or restrictions regarding 'live' contacts. We've estimated it'll take several months to piece the system back together, and within that time, more people in the A.P.U. will have seen one another in person than over the past fifty years. Certainly, you understand the significance."

He was aiming to establish liberty for the people of the A.P.U., the liberty I'd so badly sought. But I imagined how it might upset the fragile balance of the two nations' Cold War. Also, I wondered if it might cause many others from the A.P.U. to suffer the indignities that I'd now become so familiar with.

"Swiftly after," Hayden said, "will come Phase 2. Additional crates with EMP weapons will disable vast sections of the electronic fence keeping the A.P.U.'s citizens prisoner. They'll be free to defect here should they choose."

It was plainly clear to me that if I joined Hayden, I would have helped proliferate the O.A.R.'s abominable system of categorizing people, a system that had caused me so much pain.

Looking at the door, I murmured, "I don't know if I can do it."

"Janet," he said, lowering his head slightly, pointing his eyes straight at me. "Janet, please."

"I need to think about it. Can I have time to think about it?"

After a period of silence, he leaned back in his seat.

"I'll give you one week. And we'll be watching you carefully and monitoring your communications. Remember what I said about confidentiality. My assistant will tell you how to get in touch with me. One week, Janet. One week."

* * *

Days later, my friend Francisca walked with me in the rain. She was explaining to me that her family, unlike BLE and I, had entered the O.A.R. through a border that rarely accepted immigrants. She'd been young at the time but believed her father had acquiesced to sexual favors with male border security forces to get his family across the otherwise impenetrable border wall.

I was wrapped in her story but suspicious that I was being followed. I wasn't certain who was watching me. Was it one of the Category A fraternity brothers trailing me? Or was it the older man with the long hair and beard keeping pace to my right?

Suddenly, one of the Category A's from behind me lunged forward and shoved me with his hip. I tumbled onto a soaked, muddy area of the lawn. Quickly, he had his hands on me. I was terrified.

But he only wanted to roll me around in the mud. His friends laughed and cracked jokes, comparing me to a swine enjoying its own feces. Passersby paused to relish my humiliation.

The man with the long hair and beard stopped in his tracks and made brief eye contact with me. I presumed he was the tail Hayden had put on me. Unfortunately, he did nothing but watch.

Finally, the boys left me alone. Francisca pulled me out of the muck and walked me to my dorm. I'm glad I had her there, but I needed my roommate Alex. I knew she'd find a way to make me feel better.

Was I truly supposed to help these awful people with an act of O.A.R. patriotism? How could I possibly agree to help Hayden knowing that my actions could cause many others to suffer the reprehensible humiliation that I'd experienced in Category D?

At the same time, I couldn't tolerate living like this. My desire to elevate my own category couldn't have burned stronger. It was quite impossible for me to forget Hayden's offer to promote my category level in exchange for my assistance.

I tried to clear my head with a long, hot shower. Disparate thoughts ran through my mind. I was steaming with anger toward Category A and their unchallenged entitlement to do as they pleased.

Yet, I think what stung most about the incident was that the fraternity boy was so damn gorgeous! He was lean and tall. His jaw and cheekbones were solid. His eyes were dark. His full and vibrant head of hair was magnificent. I'd wanted to forgive him immediately. I grasped why the men of Category A were considered our future leaders.

But I stopped myself from waltzing down that path of thought. Soon enough, I felt self-reproach for the ease with which I'd forgiven him.

Once I was clean and dressed, I was finally able to focus upon hope. Clearly, I was in a bad situation, but I was an intelligent individual with the ability to change that.

It was imperative that I contact Hayden. In doing what he'd asked, I'd be appreciated and rewarded for applying my talents. After all, that was the very reason I'd abandoned the A.P.U. and came to the in O.A.R. in the first place! The unfortunate answer to my problem seemed obvious.

I walked out of my dorm room looking my best. I was prepared to accept Hayden's offer and practically felt elevated to Category C already.

Then, Langer stopped me in the hall. He was tearing up. "Janet," he cried my name.

I placed my hand on his arm to comfort him, and he hugged me gently.

"Thank you," he whispered. "I would've gotten clobbered."

It hadn't connected until he'd said that. I'd somehow forgotten how I'd saved Langer from Miscreant. I rubbed my hand against his back and suspected then and there that we'd be good friends for a long time.

Inside though, I heaved in fear of my own potential actions. I'd been about to betray him and Alex and all of my friends in Category D by helping Colonel Hayden and the O.A.R. proliferate its appalling system of social strata.

In that special moment with Langer, I knew I couldn't accept Hayden's offer. If anything, Category D needed to fight back.

\* \* \*

My one week to consider Hayden's offer was expiring. I hoped never to see him again so that I wouldn't have to face the awful decision he'd placed in front me.

I'd grown more depressed, wondering how my life would've unfolded had I stayed in the American Political Union. In my crate, no one could judge me, not by my gender, not by my face, and not by my body. I chastised myself daily for foolishly handing myself a miserable life.

I also considered the more painful prospect that I had no good options regardless of which nation I called home. Perhaps it was my destiny never to receive a fair chance at the life I deserved.

Prof. Houston, on the other hand, represented a unique ray of hope. He cared about all of his students regardless of category. Amazingly, I'd heard he himself was Category A.

I found his kindness and handsome looks a pleasing combination. And he was young for a professor, practically right out of graduate school.

One day during office hours, Prof. Houston was assisting me with a bonus challenge assignment. "Janet, can I ask you your category?" he inquired out of context.

I wanted to tell him. I wanted to explain the injustices I'd witnessed and experienced in the hopes that he'd understand. But at the same time, I was ashamed of my category level and didn't want him to know. Thoroughly conflicted, I couldn't get the words out.

"No need to answer," he continued. "I despise our caste system."

His noble viewpoint surprised me. Whereas I had every reason to hate our abominable system of categories, Prof. Houston, as an A, was endowed with all he needed to prosper.

I remained quiet. I remembered that Hayden might somehow be monitoring the conversation. And paranoia learned from years of A.P.U. communication-policing kept me from speaking my mind. It was difficult remembering that in the O.A.R., there were, in fact, no speech laws inhibiting free expression of one's opinion. We were free to complain about our lower status, yet most simply accepted it as the way life was meant to be.

After leaving the professor's office and upon exiting the building, I saw Hayden rapidly approaching. I considered walking the other way but knew it a lost cause. So, I stopped.

"I need an answer," he said firmly.

I didn't know how to reply. On one hand, there were strong reasons to refuse him. How could I let any more people, those now safely within the borders of the American Political Union, suffer from the O.A.R.'s system of categories? Would my friends in Category D ever forgive me?

Then, I remembered that there was nothing so great about living in an A.P.U. crate and having few real friends at all. And in accepting Hayden's offer, I could be promoted to Category B or C! Furthermore, I was afraid of Hayden and of what might become of me by failing to oblige him.

"I'll help you," I blurted, wishing that my motives were noble.

"Thank you, Janet. Your patriotism has been noted."

My apprehensions, however, didn't fade, as now I had the consequences of my actions to fear.

\* \* \*

I traveled several hundred kilometers to a location near the Old American Republic's capital city. Hayden dealt with the university so that it would accommodate my spending the second semester on an "off-campus assignment."

I joined a team of twelve engineers coding crates. We only needed to re-task thirteen crates, but twenty in total were available to us.

"What are the extra seven crates for?" I asked Grace, our team leader.

"No idea," she answered. "Maybe in case we botch a few."

Working with Grace was an honor. She was immensely sharper than I could ever have hoped to be. And of course, it was unusual for a woman to lead a technical team, especially one who wasn't a ravishing beauty.

It also occurred to me that women made up half the team. I was rather astonished that they'd have allowed such a team to exist. Perhaps Hayden was full of surprises!

\* \* \*

One afternoon several weeks in, the "secretary," as most referred to the administrative assistant, informed me that I had a visitor. I paused and followed.

She led me to a conference room where, to my surprise, BLE was waiting. Considering the circumstances with which we'd last departed, I didn't know whether to hug her or scream at her.

BLE made the decision by hugging me. The fact is, I missed her. She was a piece of my old life I wanted back.

We caught up. BLE, now Bella, attended school in the capital city and got involved with weird political groups. Embarrassed of my D-category, I hid many details of my experiences.

I suspected that I had BLE/Bella to thank in some way. She was the only one with knowledge of my technical skills with crates, and here she was. I probed her on the subject, but she was coy about it. I suspected some link between Hayden and Bella, but I couldn't put my finger on it.

* * *

The date of our EMP-weaponized crate attack on the A.P.U. was approaching. Thanks to a dedicated team, we were near ready. Somehow, I'd become so immersed in the technical challenge that I'd managed to bury my ethical qualms with the project.

Then I received another visitor, Prof. Houston. For my meeting with him, they provided a swanky conference room.

"I suppose you're wondering why I'm here," he said.

I took the comment as rhetorical and didn't respond. Yet, I wanted so much to stop being so quiet in his presence!

"The crate attack needs to be delayed," he continued.

Taken by surprise, I broke out of my bashfulness and hollered, "What? We'll be ready to go!" I didn't want the team's efforts to meet the timeline to go in vain. Also, in the back of my mind, I was restless to complete this and rise out of Category D.

"Isn't that Hayden's call?" I asked in an attempt to dismiss his logic. The professor's role in this was a mystery.

"Hayden and I are colleagues in a sense. The Colonel recruited you because Bella came forward about your crate skills at an AB-Positive meeting. I confirmed your... extraordinary talent... and tenacious spirit and—"

"AB-Positive?" I asked as his kind words made me blush.

"A political organization of Category A's and B's seeking equality reform. Our underground element intensely opposes this one-sided destructive act planned for the A.P.U."

"That doesn't make any sense! *If you wanted to stop the attack, why bring me here in the first place?*"

"Janet, you know these crates better than anyone. We need you to fabricate a technical problem that will delay the attack. Hayden will appear furious, all along knowing what you'll really be up to."

"Which is?"

"Reprogramming the last seven crates. The additional targets must be within our own country, not the A.P.U. When the attack commences and the A.P.U.'s electronic border fence goes down, so will our own border fence. People will be able to transit as they please.

"Imagine people of the O.A.R. seeing that greater equality is possible and that they don't need to accept the status quo.

"And imagine the people of the A.P.U. given back their voices... their right of open expression.

"We hope that the newfound freedom and cross-fertilization between the two nations will breed greater unity and a climate that can truly sustain human progress."

* * *

Ten years have passed since our simultaneous attacks on

the American Political Union and Old American Republic. I live with my husband, the noble professor, down the street from where I grew up. It's an easy stroll to Bella's house. Today, the neighborhood has sidewalks, which in summer, are busy with joggers, bicycles, and baby carriages. Crates are now called "cars," and they all have windows.

I haven't seen Langer and Jason since their wedding a few years ago. It's about time I visited them. They still live near the university, a long way across the country. Fortunately, travel has become easier since the reunification of the United States of America. And it's important to keep reminding myself how precious "live" friends can be.

*  *  *

*This story first appeared in the After Dinner Conversation—December 2020 issue.*

## Discussion Questions

1. Which country would you want to live in, the one with crates (*the American Political Union*) or the one with the ranking system (*the Old American Republic*)? What does it say about the personality of someone based on the community they choose?
2. When the gates opened in both directions, which country do you think had more people leave? Who do you think left from each country? What were the cultural ramifications of the bilateral exodus on each community?
3. Would the narrator have been offended by the community she migrated to (*the O.A.R.*) if she had been attractive? Didn't she change locations so she could be judged against others, or was it for another reason?
4. It seems like the narrator's main frustration was she was being judged for her looks and not her intelligence. However, to some degree, aren't both of these traits (*attractiveness and intelligence*) determined by a combination of genetics and personal effort? How do you know which traits are okay to judge a person by and which are not? Or, are all traits not suitable for judgment?
5. Could you change one of the communities to make it more acceptable while still keeping the fundamental nature of the community? If so, which one is fixable, and what would you change?

* * *

# Form Seven Alpha

*Richard Pettigrew*

\* \* \*

So here I sit with it again, Form 7α. It is printed on cheap paper with low-quality ink that smudges under my fingers. The option they judge least bad for me has been scored through, unavailable, while the four other options remain. Since the last time I faced this choice, they've updated the logo for whatever committee it is that processes these things. I sit with the cracked rubber stamp and the grimy pad of red ink. When I press the stamp into the ink and then onto the form, it will read "REQUESTED." So, which punishment should I request this time?

\* \* \*

The last time I had to complete Form 7α was a decade ago. It was my first time, and I was a different person. Two days before, I'd arrived to visit my sister, who lives on a different island from me, separated from mine by the lush, teeming forest. I crossed at night. There was me, nine other travelers, and a guide. The crossing was legal. The guide was state-approved and carried her Form 5ρ, which bore the stamp of the relevant committees. The timing was optimal, four hours after sundown, when all but two of the forest's species were asleep, and our footsteps would disturb the ecosystem minimally. The problem was me. I was illegal.

The islands were established fifty years ago. Three are residential clearings, each a thousand acres, where we live our day-to-day lives. Three are correctional clearings, only ten acres each, where we undertake any necessary punishments. Six islands in a sea of forest that totals six billion acres.

The original authorities determined that each citizen may cross from their home island to one of the other residential islands and back again at most once per year. Even this was a compromise with those who had argued there should be no crossings at any time and for any reason. We must impinge no further on the forest, they said. It must remain inviolate. But that view did not prevail. It transpires there are limits to our ecological purity. Instead, between any two islands, ten people may cross with a guide each night.

That night, I was one of the ten. The problem was that I'd already crossed that year, only two months before, in fact. That time, like this time, it was to see my sister.

\* \* \*

She's six years older than I am, and ever since I can remember, she's been the sun in my life. Every story from my childhood has her at its center: something funny she said, some game she invented, something perfect she did.

I always knew she carried a burden. Every four or five years, sometimes for months on end, a shadow would fall over her. The light would go from her eyes, the cadence from her voice, and there would be a flatness to everything she did. Part of me dreaded those months, but another part that I hated in myself welcomed them. She'd spend more time at home, more time with me, and I'd read to her late into the night.

Our mother said they'd have called it depression when she was young, but now that word means only a dip in the ground, a hollow in the earth. Our mother said they'd have given her medicine for her depression in the old world. But it wasn't talked of now—these sicknesses that show up in your mind rather than your body. We were supposed to have left them behind when we moved to the islands. They were born of a cosmic unease, they said, an unconscious, ever-present guilt about how we'd been treating the land and its creatures. They assured us this would lift when we started to live ecologically within our means, when we made our peace with the earth. But of course, it didn't. And now we had no way to talk about what my sister suffered and no way to get her any help.

Her latest bout had started as the dry season began in June. I'd sensed it approaching during our phone calls and in her letters. As soon as I was certain, I requested leave from work, telling them my sister had tripped and fallen and broken both wrists and needed help at home. They granted me two weeks, and I made the crossing the next night, my first crossing that year, all perfectly legal.

For two weeks, I read to her in the shade of an acacia tree that grew outside her living block. Always the books our mother had left for us—stories from her own childhood of things we'd never seen, like airplanes and plastic toys, telephones that you could carry in your pocket, and creatures like small black and white jaguars who would live with you in your rooms. I knew that nothing I did would shorten my sister's suffering, but perhaps my presence might temper her despair a little.

When I left, we both cried. When I returned to my island, I felt helpless. Every evening, I'd call her, but she'd say little, so I'd read to her some more. We were fast running out of stories from our mother's books. Over time, she said less and less.

I didn't know anyone in her living block. I'm certain she's popular there; she's been popular everywhere she's ever been. But no one called around when I was visiting. These things, it's understood, are kept within a family.

So when, two months after my visit, my sister stopped speaking at all on the phone and then stopped even answering, I knew I had to get back to her. But it was only August. I couldn't cross legally again until June of the following year. On the islands, years begin with the start of the dry season and end as the flood season recedes. Two seasons in each year, and I'd made my single permitted crossing for that year right at the beginning of the first.

So I stole my neighbor's identity card, made my application in his name, and received approval to cross two nights later. I couldn't request more leave from work, so I knew I could be there for only two days between shifts. Nonetheless, I had to go.

\* \* \*

The night of the crossing, the sky was clear, the moon was bright, and the heat of the day rose away from the earth. At the gate before we left, the guards checked our backpacks and handed us the headlamps we would use for the crossing. We were allowed no food while we were in the forest because it might attract the creatures, and only water to drink. The red lights of the headlamps would let us pass with minimal disturbance. The theater of our ecological sensitivity is elaborate.

Once through the checkpoint and into the forest, the path we trod was a narrow, precise groove through the stacks of moss-covered branches and piles of leaf mulch that carpeted the ground. Occasionally, our headlamps would illuminate a tree trunk that had fallen across the path during the day. If it were small enough, the guide would carefully move it to the side; if it were too large for that, we'd have to clamber over, our hands and our feet slipping on its smooth bark, which was damp from the humidity.

We walked in single file. An elderly gentleman who walked in front of me stumbled more than once, and I took his arm to steady him and reassured him silently. He nodded briefly in acknowledgment.

During long straight stretches of path, when I didn't have to concentrate on keeping my footing, my mind wandered, and I felt what I had always felt in the forest. An inexplicable urge rose in me to run off the track, deep into the tangle of ferns, and find a glade among the trees and lie perfectly still in the moonlight. Maybe my sister could come to join me there, and I could read to her as we grew old. Her depression would lift, and the light would return to her eyes. She'd invent games for us to play under the moonlight, and even now, as adults, we'd find the joy in them we found as children.

The crossing took six hours, and I wondered at times whether the elderly man ahead of me would make it. We weren't allowed to speak on the crossings, lest we should draw attention to our presence, so I couldn't learn why he was risking the journey. The authorities make very clear that these expeditions are undertaken at your own risk. They will never authorize a rescue team or send medical assistance. Only once, I'd heard, had anyone failed to complete a crossing. They were left, as promised, and only nine showed up at the gate of the receiving island that night. The following night, as people crossed that route in reverse, the body was gone, swallowed by the forest and its creatures.

As we reached the gate of my sister's island, the trees cleared, and the moon lit up our little band of exhausted travelers. There was a small cluster of people waiting to welcome us. An elderly man in a long white tunic waited to greet the man who'd been stumbling ahead of me. I watched as they embraced, and tears filled their eyes. My sister, of course, was not there, but I hadn't expected she would be.

Ten guards approached us, welcoming us and offering us bowls of beans and rice to restore our energy and water to replenish our flasks. They knew the guide and traded a few words with her, asked whether we'd encountered any creatures. No one ever did on the crossings, yet the forest retained its reputation as a place of mortal danger.

The guards fanned out, each approaching one of us in the group of crossers, smiling, asking how we'd found the journey, making pleasant inquiries about our island. The document checks were cursory, and I'd have passed undetected had it not been for the most extraordinary bad luck.

As my guard approached me, and I saw his face in the moonlight, I thought he looked familiar. Perhaps someone from my sister's living block? Someone I'd seen on my previous visit? Bad luck, for sure, but I doubted he'd remember me. Then I realized, and my stomach fell away. He was my neighbor's brother. He was a little younger, for sure, but their faces were unmistakably the same. In a rush, I remembered conversations I'd overheard between him and my neighbor on the communal telephone in the living block we shared on my island; and I remembered my neighbor afterward telling me his brother had a new job. Now I stood there in front of him, holding papers filled out in his brother's name, carrying his brother's identity card, trying to steal the single crossing his brother would be permitted that year.

The next few seconds were excruciating as I waited for realization to dawn. At first, confusion furrowed his brow as he read my permit, followed by understanding, which smoothed it again. He stepped forward and knocked me to the ground.

\* \* \*

Eighteen hours later, I was standing at a different gate, waiting to make another crossing, this time to the smallest of the three correctional islands. After I'd been pulled roughly to my feet by two other guards from where my neighbor's brother had floored me, I'd been detained in a small shed next to the entrance gate. It was stacked with shovels and buckets, tarpaulins and wooden boards, presumably stored here in anticipation of the flood season, when the ground on the islands would turn to soup.

At one point, a guard I didn't recognize opened the door to ask me whether my neighbor knew that I was crossing in his name. I said he didn't. I explained that I'd stolen the identity card. She slammed the door shut without another word.

It transpired later that they'd got a judge on the telephone and were conducting a cursory trial among themselves. Since I was admitting all wrongdoing, they didn't seem to think anything more was required, and the judge agreed. After another few hours passed, I was told the verdict. I would cross to Correctional Island C3, where I'd be given Form 7α. That would present me with my options.

When the time came to cross, I was unaccompanied, as all prisoners are. You commit your crime alone, and you face your punishment alone, and no guard's life will be risked crossing between islands with you. Besides, there was nowhere to run. The narrow path I followed that night was walled in on either side by great vines covered with a hundred types of moss and vast fallen palms that stretched out across the forest's floor like mile-high pins knocked down in a bowling alley. The forest was impenetrable.

I made the crossing in three hours. As I reached the gate to the correctional island, my water canteen was empty, and my feet ached. My welcome was polite, gentle, almost kind, but a little weary and impersonal, as if the lines were learned by rote, which I'm sure they were. The custodians on these islands are proud to take their titles literally. They are there not to inflict your punishment on you but to assist you in undertaking it yourself. Just as a forest guide helps you cross, a custodian helps you atone. But unlike the guides, they don't endure the experience with you.

\* \* \*

After refilling my canteen, the gentle man who had welcomed me took me to a small room in a long, low building by the gate and handed me Form 7α, a little red ink pad, and a rubber stamp. The options in the list were presented using cryptic euphemisms, but we all knew what they meant. We all learned our civic history at knowledge gatherings in our childhood, and as adults, we passed it on to the next generation in the same way.

\* \* \*

### *Option 1. Induced sleep. Duration: two seasons.*

During the year for which this punishment lasts, your consciousness is simply switched off. You lie on a bed in the island's infirmary, and two cannulas are placed in the veins that run up the inside of your forearms. Through one, flow the chemicals that, for two full seasons, keep you in a dreamless sleep; through the other, flow the nutrients and fluids that keep you alive. Custodians move you gently each day to avoid bed sores, and occasionally they stand you upright as a prophylactic against some unspecified condition you might develop. You're unaware of it all.

The grand theory of our new correctional techniques was devised fifty years ago when the islands were first inhabited. It states our collective intention that this option should be painless. The punishment it offers entails no suffering. You simply lose a year of your conscious life. In reality, those who had experienced it said the physical rehabilitation you need after you leave the infirmary is torture, your withered muscles trying to regain their strength, your body adjusting to being vertical again.

In any case, the option was scored through on my form: unavailable. In theory, they score through the option they think the prisoner will prefer. Like so many features of our lives, this was a compromise with the hardliners among the original settlers, who had felt it made a mockery of the purpose of punishment to allow the prisoner any say at all in its nature. In reality, however, I suspect they removed this option for me simply because they didn't want me out of the workforce for a whole year and then useless and weak for a further season as my body recovered.

\* \* \*

### *Option 2. Elevated productivity. Duration: one season.*

In every society that attempts to eschew hierarchy and privilege and live together as equals, there arises the question of those tasks so repellent that no one wants to do them. For our islands, as for so many such communities, they are the processing of sewage and the disposal of the dead. Were it not for our ecological austerity, we might dispose of both in the forest, the first to nourish the plants and beetles, the second to feed the carrion birds and the carnivores. But that is not our ethos. We neither add anything to the forest nor extract anything from it.

In the early days, some suggested that this detested work should be done by everyone, perhaps allocated on a schedule, so that for five days in each season, this would be your job. Others thought there would be sufficient volunteers provided certain extra privileges were offered as an inducement: an extra crossing per year, perhaps, or a stipend on top of your salary. But the policy that prevailed was that prisoners would do it. So it was added to Form 7α as an option. And for me, it remained available.

\* \* \*

### *Option 3. Extended solitude. Duration: half season.*

My mother had told us that, in the old world, prisoners would call this "the box" or "the hole," and custodians would call it "secure housing," and it might last tens of years. By any name, and for whatever duration, for us it means complete isolation in a small windowless one-roomed hut that is raised on stilts above the ground. The room contains an electric light, a mattress, a toilet, and a hatch. The walls are a dull white of the sort that looks dirty even when it's freshly painted. From the hatch, you retrieve the meals that the custodians bring you; a small green light above it indicates when one is available. The room is soundproofed so that you can neither talk with the custodians through the hatch nor hear the sounds of the forest around you. Nor, indeed, can the custodians hear any sounds you are moved to make in your solitude. As a result, when they open the door of a hut at the end of a sentence, they don't know what they might find. This option, too, was available to me.

\* \* \*

### *Option 4. Enhanced displeasure. Duration: one week.*

The shortest punishment, this was also the most feared. From what I've heard, it is always made available on Form 7α but almost never chosen. Like the box, it is undertaken in a small room in a soundproofed hut. Every morning at dawn for seven mornings in a row, a custodian arrives and injects your upper arm with a clear liquid. After five minutes, the pain floods in, consumes your whole body, and stays at a constant, quivering fever pitch until dusk, when the custodian returns with a second injection that relieves it. Then you go to bed and await the following day. For me, as for everyone, this was available.

\* \* \*

### *Option 5. Reduced privilege. Duration: in perpetuity.*

This was available to me as it usually is to anyone young and reasonably healthy. For those nearer to death, it is not considered a sufficient punishment, though from the beginning, some had asked what we thought we were achieving by punishing them anyway. I could choose this option and walk straight off the correctional island and return home. My identity card would be marked with a small orange dot in the upper right-hand corner. Nothing more. I'd only start to feel the effects gradually. When I applied to make a crossing, and my application was denied with no reason given; when some undesirable task would become necessary on my island, and I'd find myself added to the list of the volunteers without volunteering; when I saw my name at the bottom of the list for the communal telephone every time I asked to use it, and never on the list at all when any excess food became available. A lifetime of small, unpredictable degradations and frustrations.

That option completed the list. The first was scored through, and I must choose from the remaining four. If I didn't, if I refused to make the choice, the custodians would choose on my behalf at random, and the duration of the selected punishment would triple. I picked up the little stamp, pressed it into the ink pad, and marked the third option: Option 3: Extended solitude. Duration: half season. "REQUESTED."

* * *

My first day in the box was the first time I really reflected on my situation. From the moment my neighbor's brother had discovered my crime, through the detention in the hut, the crossing, and then my arrival on the correctional island, I'd been in a haze, my mind deferring all thought until a later, more stable time. But inside the box, after the door closed and the custodian left, there was nothing further to wait for except my release in three months' time.

The absence of all sounds except the ones you make

yourself is unsettling at first, but it wasn't entirely unfamiliar to me. Sometimes, as a child, if I was awake and my sister wasn't snoring, if the rest of the living block was asleep and the forest had fallen silent, I'd enjoy the noiseless tranquility and wish it would last longer.

I thought of my sister now. I hadn't told her I'd be coming to visit, so she wouldn't be expecting me, but she'd surely expect my phone call in the evening, and she'd worry when it didn't come the first night, then the second, and then on and on. News of punishments spread quickly on the islands, but she'd become completely cut off from her living block, so it would take some time to reach her.

I thought of her worries about me pushing her deeper into her darkness, and it caused me a dull, deadening pain. She was condemned to her own solitude now. No one would read her stories in the evenings; no one would try to coax her out of the dark corners where her mind led her; no one was there to tug on that line that reached down into the deep black waters where she was currently suspended, easing her inch by inch back toward the surface.

That thudding, throbbing pain never left me my whole time inside that box. It became a constant companion, there when I switched off the light and slept, and there again when I woke. It was there in every dream I had.

I had imagined the chief horror that solitude would hold would be the absence of any stimulus from outside. And that surely is a horror, and it surely caused me great anguish. But solitude also robs you of agency, and I hadn't accounted for that. Just as the outside world cannot impinge on you, you can do nothing to change the outside world. I couldn't call my sister, couldn't write to her; I couldn't send word that I was well, or at least alive, couldn't tell her I'd be reading stories to her again on the telephone before long. And without that feeling that I was doing something to improve things for her, the pain I felt because of the pain I knew she felt stayed, stubbornly unchanging, the same shape sitting in my gut from the start until near the end when it morphed into something far worse.

But, before that, there was something else to face, for I quickly realized that the mind is held together more by external forces than by inner strength. And what the box most surely removes are external forces.

For so long, I'd harbored this illicit dream of running off into the forest to find solitude. Away from the noise of the living block, away from the tedium of my work shifts, away from the neighbors and friends who want to bend my ear to complain about their partners or gossip about their relatives. Away from the constant little taps, prods, and nudges that the social world inflicts every day. And yet, there inside that box for half a season with the green light that signaled mealtimes as the only intrusion from the outside world, I realized how much I needed those taps and prods and nudges. My mind, waking from sleep each day, set off ideas running like a pack of mice released from a sack. Off they'd scurry, and soon some would be approaching perilous areas. Outside the box, I'd get distracted before any idea could go too far out of bounds. The distraction would slow it down, maybe remove it altogether, or set it on a better course. It would do the same with the good thoughts, too, of course, slow them down, remove them sometimes, and that's what made me long for solitude, somewhere to let the good thoughts run their full distance. But in the box, with no distractions—nothing to impinge on my consciousness—it wasn't the good thoughts that were freed to follow their course but the bad ones, which reached deeper and deeper into the dangerous areas of my mind.

In the old world, my mother had told us, the box was not soundproofed, and prisoners held there would hear the custodians talk, and they'd hear the other inmates gibber and scream as their minds unraveled, and they'd pray it wouldn't happen to them. When the penal code for our islands was written, it was thought more humane to soundproof the huts. But what looks less barbaric to those who've never experienced it very often isn't. Within two weeks, I was screaming at the walls that I wanted to change my choice on Form 7α. I wanted the needle and the pain it brought. Surely no thought was possible in the midst of that agony. Surely that would stop me from thinking.

*  *  *

By the end of the first month, I became seriously concerned about the state of mind in which I'd leave the box. I'd once heard stories of a man who couldn't be alone after his time inside. Even the hubbub and jostling of the living blocks weren't enough for him. He needed to always talk. He wore down friend after friend and lover after lover with his insatiable need for contact. He became a beggar, not for money because we had none of that, but for company.

I'd also met a woman who'd started to hallucinate in here and couldn't stop after she'd been released. Her mind had created companions for her. At first, she could hear them only, their voices seeming to come from the walls; but gradually, they assumed bodies, dressed in clothes, and sat beside her to talk.

She described their clothes to me one day as long tunics with elaborate embroidery. As she talked, her eyes stared past me at something a little way off. When I turned to look, it was an empty space.

I couldn't let this happen to me, so I tried to devise a strict regimen to keep my mind intact. I had no pencil or paper, so I couldn't write them down, but perhaps I could make up stories and tell them to myself as if I were telling them to my sister. Then I'd have something to share with her when we saw each other again. But the stories soon became overwrought, tangled, a profusion of detail and spandrels and tangents, obsessively pursued. As before, my mind simply could not supply on its own the boundaries, the myriad pushbacks, and corrections that any listener besides me might have provided. The mice, unconstrained, just ran where they would.

My next plan was to slow my thought processes. On Form 7α, the option that offers induced sleep lasts four times as long as the option that offers the box, an acknowledgment that having no consciousness at all, being as it were in a temporary death, is to be preferred to being conscious in this soundless solitude. So I aimed to bring my mind as close to sustained unconsciousness as it would let me.

I found I couldn't force myself to sleep for most of the day, and as I tried to sleep longer and longer, my dreams became more and more like the tangled, tortured stories I'd been telling myself before.

My mother had told us once of something her parents used to do in the old world. They'd sit, a group of strangers in a circle, and just breathe. As thoughts would arrive in their mind, they'd simply observe them, dismiss them, and return their attention to their breath. So I tried that. After a few days, it began to work, and I enjoyed some respite from my thoughts. But now the pendulum swung to its other extreme, which was boredom. At first, I welcomed it. To be bored after a month of frenetic, unloosed thoughts was bliss. I felt my whole body melt into the blankness of my mind, and I'd lose myself for hours on end. But true boredom, sustained over time, is not how you imagine. You think it will be an absence. But in reality, it becomes a real, substantial thing, like a thick tarry liquid that builds in your stomach and rises through your chest cavity and stands in your throat, ready to choke you.

\* \* \*

The mind will only tolerate so much stasis, or at least mine will. As I entered my final month in the box, the mania of the thoughts returned, and all my attempts to dismiss them did not work. It was at this time that the pain I felt because of my sister's suffering grew, changed shape, and threatened to undo me. Through the final month, my mind was clenched not just by pain but also by guilt.

The thought haunted me that I had done this to her. Because of me, she had spent two months already in complete solitude, cut off from me and from her living block, and another month lay ahead. I was to blame for that. That gave a twist to the pain that was already there and had been there constantly throughout the past two months. It brought it fully to life, made it hum in my abdomen as if there was an electric current running through it. Pain, with a buzzing electric corona of guilt. I had been rash. I'd made a half-baked plan that was unlikely to succeed, and I'd got myself caught. *But you did it for me*, I heard my sister say in my head, and in the perfect silence of the room, the words sounded loud enough to be real, and I thought of the woman who could not shake her hallucinations. But I wondered whether my sister was right about this. Had I truly done it selflessly? Or was I not simply trying to recover something—her—that was so crucial to my own happiness?

But still, there was more to feed my guilt. More and worse. After all, I had chosen this option, three months of solitude. I could have chosen a week of chemical pain instead. That was available to me on my Form 7α. If I'd chosen that, I would have been free seven weeks ago. I would have been able to call her every evening for the past seven weeks. Instead, I would be leaving my sister an extra eleven weeks alone, and I did it because I was too frightened of their needle and the pain it would deliver.

You think your love is unconditional. Form 7α disabused me of that.

It was this, among everything else that happened in there, that came closest to breaking me. I couldn't dislodge the thought. I was the author of all this. No one but me bore any responsibility for it. I had sent my sister into the deepest solitude at exactly the time when she was least able to bear it. Like a Catherine wheel firework, the guilt spun in my mind, its sparks touching every corner, singeing wherever they landed.

Form 7α was to be a centerpiece of our new egalitarian society. When you err, there is no authority above you who chooses your punishment, no executioner who metes it out. The choice is yours, and the custodians are there only to assist—stagehands who set the scene and pass you the props. As the final days of my time in the box dragged on, and I found myself crouching in the corner of the hut, clenching my hair in my fists, the deep anguish of my guilt always on the cusp of overwhelming me, I wondered whether those who had created that form had ever imagined what it would do.

\* \* \*

No one talks much of the custodians who staff these correctional islands. As with the job of judge and gate guard, this is not a vocation for which you can apply in our society. Rather, you are approached if the relevant committee thinks you might be suitable. If they deem you kind, resilient, fair, in general, virtuous, then they will ask you to consider this post. The joke goes that if you don't want the job, it's yours. But this presents a paradox. Those invited to become custodians are those least likely to agree, and we never compel anyone to do work they do not wish to do. Unless they're prisoners, of course. So they are enticed partly with longer periods of leave and earlier dates for retirement but also with a reverence paid communally by all the people of our society. While we do not talk of them often, the custodians know that they are esteemed. The committee has deemed them virtuous people, and we together respect that judgment. It's surprising, or surprising to me, the power of our fellows' esteem in a society like ours.

When my custodian opened the door of my hut to release me on the final day of my sentence, what I noticed first were the sounds. A flock of blue macaws swept overhead and turned as one rippling entity, banking west, and the swish of their feathers and the scream of their calls filled my ears, the first sound not of my own making that I'd heard for three months. They disappeared toward the setting sun, which was beginning to fill the sky with its colors, as if orange and purple ink was seeping into blue blotting paper, creeping across it. As their calls receded, I heard the gentle background buzz of the insects that live near the forest's edge and the light flutter of the leaves in the trees brushing against one another.

What I noticed second, after the sounds and the sky, was the custodian's face. It betrayed a sort of wariness, and his body looked tensed in anticipation of trouble. He would have none from me, and I smiled quickly and thanked him to signal that I bore him no ill will. It stayed with me, though, the learned caution that his look betrayed. I wondered what he had seen before when he'd opened that door.

Two hours after my release, I was taken to the gate on the other side of the correctional island from the one where I'd entered. My canteen was filled with fresh water, and my custodian set me on my way back to my home island with a tired smile and a hackneyed joke about hoping never to see me again while he was at work. I smiled in return, strapped on the red headlamp he gave me, and began my journey. Island C3, where I spent my solitude, lies halfway between my sister's island and my own, and I arrived at the gates to mine in a little under four hours. While I'd tried to keep active in the box, there is a limit to what's possible. So, as I trekked through the thick oozing mud and tripped on the hidden ferns that crisscrossed the forest path, my legs were weak, and I had to stop a number of times and rest on a vine branch to catch my breath.

As I reentered my island through the gate I had left illegally three months before, I felt that strange dislocation that occurs when you find a place familiar but know the person through whose eyes you saw it before is not the person you've become who sees it now. I made my way across the island to my living block as the sun started to rise. As I got closer and closer to my neighborhood, I knew more and more of the people I passed. They were leaving for work as I was returning home, and they greeted me warmly. I would go to work again tomorrow morning, but today I was given to acclimatize.

We pride ourselves here on treating Form $7\alpha$ as the last word on a person's punishment. Once you have undertaken whatever sentence you choose from it, your crime is of no further consequence. Your debt is paid, and you return to society to be treated exactly as you were before. We have agreed, collectively, that these punishments are sufficient and no further sanction is required; we believe, collectively, that a crime teaches us nothing of the perpetrator's character and everything about the contingencies that might land any one of us in their position. Individually, of course, many of us dissent from this opinion.

So, as I entered my living block, I was greeted by my neighbors as if I had hardly left. As I approached the door to my living space, I noticed it was ajar, and a pair of sandals sat neatly arranged outside. I assumed it was a friend who'd come by to open my rooms and let out the stagnant air that must have built up while they lay empty. But when I pushed the door open, I saw instead my sister sitting in the wicker chair by the window, her head resting on a cushion, her eyes closed, and her hands holding one another loosely in her lap. As I gently shut the door, she awoke, and I could see immediately that the shadow had lifted from her mind, and her eyes once again held that special light that shone through so many of my childhood memories. Her face, soft and blank in sleep, broke into a grin as she woke up, half mischievous, half apprehensive, looking at me and knowing that we had both endured so much since we were last able to laugh together and wondering whether it had robbed us of the chance to do so again.

* * *

Even now, from the far vantage point of the future, I find it hard to describe the next three days we spent together. I can say how we spent our time, of course. On the first day, my sister cooked for us the meal my mother had always made on our birthdays. "As close to decent, old-world food as you can get out here," she used to say, and my sister mimicked her voice as she served it up for us in my rooms, and we both laughed. That night we talked about our mother until the sun set, and we went to sleep. My sister walked with me to work in the morning and met me there again at the end of my shift, and we walked along the fence that separated the island from the forest and watched a flock of macaws overhead and an army of ants underfoot. Then I cooked for her, and we fell asleep as the sun set again. The third day was the same, except that my neighbors dropped in as we were finishing dinner. Some had met my sister on previous visits; others, I think, were just curious because they knew I'd gone to the box for trying to visit her.

So, yes, I can tell the events of these days well enough. But the emotions that ran through them are much less clear to me.

On the first night, about halfway from sunset to sunrise, I was shaken out of sleep by a nightmare in which I was stranded alone in the forest. I turned over and looked up to see my sister at the window crying, the tears on her cheek catching the moonlight. I said nothing, and in time she lay down again. I think we both remained awake until the sun rose, and it was time for me to leave for work. By then, she was smiling and joking and asking what we should make for dinner.

As the sun set on her final day, she prepared her backpack for the crossing back to her home island. We walked over to the gate together. The same guards were on duty who had unwittingly let me pass illegally that night three months ago. One of them stiffened when they saw me, but the others paid me no attention. My sister and I embraced, and she said to me, low and choked, her voice cracking, "I'm so sorry you ever had to make that choice." I didn't reply. I couldn't begin to think how I should. She turned and left through the gate.

\* \* \*

For the next decade, we visited one another each year for however long our work would grant us leave. We adhered to the law, each of us crossing just once every two seasons. My sister's depression fell into a long remission, and I began to wonder whether she was free of it completely. But in the ninth year, it returned, and I started to think instead that it would never leave again.

History repeated itself with small changes. I made one crossing at the beginning of the year, just as the flood season gave way to the dry. I found my sister in a desperate state. I crossed back but knew I couldn't remain another two seasons without seeing her again. As the evening phone calls became harder and harder to bear, I knew the time was approaching when I would have to try again.

I made it further this time than last. I made the crossing, I was waved through by the guards on my sister's island, and I even managed to spend the last two days with her before they found me. It seems a neighbor reported yesterday that I was missing from my living block. They haven't told me who it was, and I guess they never will, but I suspect I know.

\* \* \*

So here I sit again with Form 7α, the little rubber stamp, and the pad of red ink. At this moment ten years ago, I made a choice that taught me something I never wanted to know. This time, I won't let it teach me anything at all.

My custodian returns to the room and asks for the form, and I hand it back. She looks at it and sees I've left it blank. She looks at me and frowns a little. She starts to return it to me. She opens her mouth to explain how the system works, that if I don't make a choice, she'll choose at random, and the duration will triple. I shake my head and raise my palm to stop her, for I know all that. After a moment, she nods and leaves the room. I exhale and sit back to wait while she determines my sentence.

\* \* \*

*This story first appeared in the After Dinner Conversation—October 2023 issue.*

## Discussion Questions

1. If you were forced to fill out the punishment form, which punishment would you choose and why?
2. Do you think the various punishment options are roughly equal, or are certain ones worse/better? What makes them so?
3. Why did the narrator leave his punishment form blank at the end of the story?
4. Are certain rational and reasonable crimes, like illegally traveling to visit a suffering family member, moral? Or are laws meant to impose a collective benefit but an individual loss? Was the narrator right to break the law?
5. The society in the story believes "a crime teaches us nothing of the perpetrator's character and everything about the contingencies that might land any one of us in their position." What does this mean, and do you agree or disagree?

\* \* \*

# Euthanasia

*Kelly Piner*

\* \* \*

On a frigid December morning, Hank Sanders stomped the caked mud off his worn boots and entered Discount Hardware. He couldn't shake his cousin's remarks. *Put her down*, he'd said. The words had rolled so effortlessly off his lips, as if her life meant nothing at all, as if, simply by being old, she'd become too much trouble.

Hank marched up one aisle and down another, searching for a new blade for his knife. When had the shelves become so barren? It hadn't looked like this the last time he'd shopped there. But with the fuel shortages and the lack of truckers, was it any wonder? And where was everyone? He hadn't seen any other customer or any staff. With no one to help him find the blade or even care if he made a purchase, he returned to his old pickup, trash crunching under his boots.

He drove south, thirty miles along the Ohio River, where sheets of fog hovered over the water and worn concrete road. As he squinted and leaned into the wheel, he choked down his sense of loss for his nation. Once an abundant land of plenty, it now resembled a third-world nation with food and energy shortages. Little by little, residents were adjusting to lack and uncertainty. Incredible, he thought, how easily people could be conditioned to accept less and less.

At the fenced compound, he punched the access code into the keyboard, and a gate slid open, exposing a comforting wrought-iron sign that read: *House of Hope: Where Your Suffering Ends*. That sign had greeted him for as long as he could remember. In stark contrast, the massive gray government structure stood cold and uninviting just beyond the gate.

He drove to the back entrance and mentally prepared for another twelve-hour day. When he climbed from his truck, he avoided looking at the blurry mounds spread out on the grass. Through the darkness, he spotted a new shipment of crates that had been delivered during the night. It never ended.

Inside, he said, "Hi, girl," and bent over to pet the blue point Siamese that greeted him.

He'd often felt that Ling Ling had the gift of second sight, the way she seemed to sense the fear and dying spirits of those about to be put down and did her best to comfort them.

Hank flipped on the overhead fluorescent lights, and they made a hissing sound like that of a final breath being expelled. The sterile, concrete warehouse had no windows on the main floor. The only windows were in Hank's office on the second floor, facing the large cemetery out back. Some days, when he'd been outside digging holes for the smaller creatures, he could have sworn that he'd felt dead eyes staring at him. Just how many had he put down over the years? He refused to count. So many that the cemetery was full.

He checked his clipboard. Forty to dispose of today. He'd never gotten used to it, the death and misery he'd witnessed during his ten years running House of Hope, but he didn't want to think about that. Instead, he steeled himself and went about doing his morning inspection, going from one cell to another.

He donned a mask and entered the ice locker where the deceased rested, awaiting processing. It, too, was so full that now he arranged the overflow bodies on the ground by the cemetery. He checked his calendar. The eighteen-wheeler had last collected the corpses over two weeks ago. The crew had used a conveyor belt to move the dead bodies inside the trailer where they were stacked. What happened to them afterward, he didn't want to know.

In Euthanasia Cell Block No. 1, twenty dogs awaited euthanasia. However much he disinfected the cages between each use, they still smelled of death, and the animals all yelped for his help. He reached down and handfed a chicken-flavored treat to a toy poodle. Did the dogs understand that their owners had elected to put them down? And how many were really suffering, as opposed to having worn out their welcome through aging? No longer adorable puppies, many now required ongoing care as elderly pets.

And of course, the pet food shortage didn't help. Owners had grown tired of the weekly search all over town for dog food. Even here, the government refused to pay for pet food. The animals were being put down anyway, so why throw money away? But Hank refused to let the creatures suffer, so he purchased food out of his own pocket. He didn't mind the extra running around.

A chocolate Labrador, beautiful and bouncy, stuck his

paw outside his cage and cried. Hank opened the cage and petted the dog's head. "Who'd put you down?" he asked the distraught animal. He passed each cage and spoke kindly to every dog. It was the least he could do.

*Put her down*, played over in Hank's head like an endless tape loop. The knot in his chest tightened when he entered Cell Block No. 2, the feline room. He'd had a special fondness for cats ever since his mother had given him a marmalade kitten for his fourth birthday, and Hank had slept with Dylan every night of the cat's life. Now, a newly arrived marmalade, just like Dylan, whined when Hank approached, and he scratched the cat's neck. "It'll be okay, boy. I'd take you home if I could." He put the cat onto the floor, and Ling Ling rushed over and washed his ears.

In the beginning, Hank's dad had built a welcoming barn for the creatures they would take home. He'd even installed heat to keep them comfortable during the frigid mid-Western winters. But that had ended years ago with the government's No Removal Laws, forbidding euthanasia contractors from rescuing animals. Too many lives were unaccounted for, the government had said. Oversight was necessary for the welfare of the community. So now they kept strict inventory, and a hefty euthanasia tax paid for the centers.

His father had been the first operator hired by the government over twenty years ago. A soft-hearted man, his passion had been to humanely lay all forms of life to rest, however big or small. His dying wish had been that Hank would carry on the business.

Unlike his father, Hank didn't remember a time when the private medical sector handled these matters in their small practices. Still, when he had accompanied his dad to work, families hadn't simply dropped off a loved one to be euthanatized. They had delivered them kindly, with tearful goodbyes. But new laws had banished families from the compound. To make the whole process less personal, Hank figured, so families could more easily walk away.

He sometimes wished he could walk away too, but if he did, he'd have no way of knowing how the new operator would treat the "inventory." Most days, he wondered if he served any valuable function at all, beyond showing a bit of kindness to every poor soul brought to the facility.

Outside, he cranked up the forklift and moved first one crate and then another into the warehouse. When he'd moved the last one, he used a crowbar to open the first crate, smaller than the others. Inside lay a hodgepodge of tiny rabbits, guinea pigs, and lizards, all shivering from being left outside overnight. At least their owners hadn't just abandoned them on the side of the road, as millions of others were abandoned each year.

Hank rolled a heat lamp over to warm them. He saw no reason they shouldn't be kept comfortable during their final moments. He lifted a trembling bunny and wrapped her in a soft fleece blanket. In the past, he had occasionally broken the rules and had taken an animal home, despite the risk. If he'd gotten caught, he would have faced not only stiff fines but criminal charges, and he would have lost his license as operator of House of Hope. Since the enactment of the government's surveillance program, his every move was filmed, making it impossible to rescue defenseless creatures, so instead, he moved the menagerie into Cell Block No. 3.

As he had done for the past ten years, he prepared the supplies to euthanize the first group. As always, he avoided eye contact as he lifted a trembling dachshund from her cage and inserted the intravenous catheter into her leg. "I'm here with you, girl. It'll be okay," he said softly. Next, he injected a sedative to relax her. "Our Father who art in heaven," he recited before he inserted the death serum into her vein.

One by one, Hank moved down the line, avoiding eye contact as he inserted the death serum. He ended the procession with the Labrador, which he cradled in his arms as the dog gasped his last breath. Then, he moved the corpses outside onto the grass, where the cold temperatures would preserve their bodies until pickup later. He ran his gaze over the expansive grounds, where no fewer than five hundred creatures lay as if sleeping.

He hadn't known it would be this way when his dad had trained him as the next operator. The loneliness and isolation. But his father had pounded a strong work ethic into him, and Hank often worked seven days a week, carrying out his father's last wishes. He had never married. It wouldn't have been fair, being away from home so much. Ling Ling was his only constant companion during the endless days and nights when he elected to sleep on his cot.

"Ling Ling," he called, and the Siamese rushed up, meowing. "Come inside with Daddy." His hand trembled when he placed it on the knob of the main euthanasia room, Cell Block No. 4. He had unloaded four crates into the room earlier, and he took a deep breath before using the crowbar to remove the first lid under the watchful gaze of the blue electronic eye in the ceiling. It was always the same, the shock.

Inside lay an emaciated man, identified as Subject No. 36, age seventy-five. The old man's lips trembled as he struggled to speak. Hank leaned down, but no words of comfort would come. Did he have an incurable disease, or was the family just tired of caring for him? He'd never know, so he focused on inserting the catheter into the man's frail arm. He avoided looking into the elderly man's eyes, lest he be identified as the bad guy, the executioner.

It had once been an honorable institution, the euthanasia centers, after the new right-to-die laws were passed. No more lingering for months in cancer wards or in unsanitary nursing homes, barely remembering one's name. Finally, the sick could choose to end their suffering. In the beginning, patients and families met with a trusted physician, and together they made the best decision. But as with most well-intentioned programs, greed and corruption eventually got their fingers into the pot. Little by little, the dignities were chipped away until one day— he couldn't remember how it had happened—the trucks started delivering flimsy wooden containers. Supply chain shortages, the government had said. Crates, inhumane and barbaric, were plentiful and cheap, and no need to tie up limited emergency vehicles transporting those who would only be put down anyway. With too few resources and too many souls on the planet eating up limited supplies, especially the infirm and old, a single family member could elect to put someone down with only one federal physician required to sign off on the procedure. Now the sick and helpless were being shipped out like expired produce. How much worse it could get? He was afraid to guess.

Tears rolled down the old guy's face as Hank recited the Lord's Prayer for him. It was the least he could do to send the old man off with a little dignity.

In the next crate, a sixty-nine-year-old woman barely had a pulse. Her legs had already been amputated. Diabetes, Hank thought. He inserted the catheter and injected the death serum. He saw this as a blessing, ending her suffering. Maybe she had loved ones waiting for her on the other side. He could hope.

Hank removed the lid from the third crate. "Granny!" he shrieked.

Inside, his eighty-five-year-old grandmother, wrapped in only a flimsy white sheet, was identified as Subject No. 78. So much adrenaline shot through him, he could barely feel his body. *Put her down*, his cousin had said.

With bones as brittle as rotting wood, she looked as if she might turn to sawdust if he hugged her too hard. Her cheekbones and blue veins protruded through translucent skin. Gone was the luxuriant red hair she had always neatly arranged in a bun. Now, her nearly bald scalp showed through thin, gray hair. Still, her hazel eyes shone with kindness. Underneath the sheet, she wore only the pink flannel nightgown he had given her for her last birthday. Even in this state, she forced a smile, the crevices around her eyes as deep as tunnels.

His grandmother's face came in and out of focus, and a flood of emotions tore through him—disbelief, despair, guilt. He shut his eyes, praying it was all a bad dream. But when he opened them, he heard, "Dear God," as if a voice had come from outside himself.

Hank's mother had died of cancer when he'd been just five, and his dad had moved Grandma Kitty in to live with them. For him, she was more a mother than a grandmother. She had sugar cookies waiting for him when he returned from school, and she'd attended all his high school football games, sitting in the bleachers with a homemade afghan thrown over her legs. Hank had learned his love of animals from her as much as from his father. She had never turned away a stray and had volunteered her time at the local animal shelter where she'd taken Hank on weekends as a boy. "They give you unconditional love and exist on a higher spiritual plane," she'd said. Even as a child, Hank had understood what she meant. Now, as if sensing her love for animals, Ling Ling jumped inside the crate, purring and butting her head against Granny's cheek.

Could he have prevented this if he'd worked less and had spent more time with her?

He steadied himself against the crate and stroked her wiry hair. "Granny, who sent you here?" She'd gone to live with his Aunt Betty last year after she'd fallen and broken her hip. He could imagine Aunt Betty sending her away for extermination. She didn't even have time for her own children.

Granny gazed into his eyes and tried to speak. Just like the rabbit before her, she trembled from the cold as Hank tucked a soft blanket around her.

"I'm here to help you," he said, desperate to assuage his guilt and to make things right. He leaned down and kissed her cheek. But who was he kidding? He glanced up at the camera in the ceiling, ever watching. She knew what he did at the warehouse. He could see it in her eyes.

In all his years here, this was the first time he'd ever come face-to-face with a relative. He'd once put down a neighbor who'd been eaten up with cancer and then a teenager who'd lived on his street after the boy had been mangled beyond repair in a car crash. But this?

He closed his eyes and prayed for strength. So this was all

his granny's life was worth after she'd given so much of herself?

To hell with it, he thought. For a split second, he thought he'd rescue her. But then what? If he tried to save her, the authorities would catch up to them before he'd even make it home. He'd be taken away, jailed, and some stranger would unmercifully exterminate her.

She grasped his hand in her tiny, bony appendage and somehow conveyed her acceptance. It's all right, she seemed to be saying as she held his gaze. He steeled himself. The past ten years had prepared him for this moment. Even if no one believed it but himself, he served a valuable function. Treating every creature at the center with love and respect was his calling, his passion. Without a doubt, he provided the last glimmer of kindness any of them would ever know.

He leaned down closer, still looking directly into Granny's eyes. His voice cracked. "You're the best grandmother a boy could ever have had. I'm here to help you move into the light. I have to believe it will be peaceful and beautiful. Your suffering will end, and Grandpa will be waiting for you. Is there anything you want to say?"

Her lips barely moved, but her eyes conveyed the same love they always had.

Hank had the sensation of leaving his body as he quietly inserted the catheter into her arm. "Our Father who art in Heaven," he recited, and without guilt, he lifted the death serum and inserted it into her vein.

* * *

*This story first appeared in the After Dinner Conversation—August 2023 issue.*

## Discussion Questions

1. What, if any, scarcity scenario would justify this kind of treatment for loved pets and the elderly? How bad would things have to get (*if ever*) for this to be okay?
2. What aspects of the euthanizing process are most offensive to you; being shipped in boxes, being barred from seeing loved ones in their final moments, being left in the cold, being left alone, being euthanized at all, or something else?
3. The story seems to imply the world situation deteriorated very rapidly, making the care of pets and elderly family members prohibitively expensive. Given the new global reality, what, if any, regulations would you put in place for having children or buying new pets in the future? Do people have an inalienable right to own a pet, have a child, and choose when they die?
4. The narrator justifies his role in this process by saying he, unlike others, treats those he is about to euthanize with dignity. Is this a better option than nonparticipation in an unjust system? Does the narrator believe the system is unjust or simply tragic?
5. What would you do if you were the narrator in this story?

\* \* \*

# Author Information

## The Book Of Approved Words

**W.M. Pienton** is influenced by John Bellairs, H. P. Lovecraft, Lord Dunsany, and Neil Gaiman. Along with writing he likes drawing and occasionally playing guitar (poorly). When relaxing he likes a good whiskey or scotch. Sometimes he sits on the porch smoking his pipe and watches the world go past.

## The Draft

**Jan McCleery** spent her career as a software engineer start-up founder, and applies her independent woman experiences in a man's world to her writing and thought processes. Jan became a California Delta activist and formed a nonprofit to fight the "water wars." Jan has also published nine books, including her recent spy novel series. *www.FromTheDuckPond.com*

## For Your Safety

**Ty Lazar** works as a software developer in Alberta, Canada. Lately, he's been spending his time reading and writing science fiction when he should be preparing for grad school, where he plans to study artificial intelligence. "For Your Safety" is his first published work.

## Understanding Ice Cream

**Earl Smith** is a political and social theorist with a PhD in Political and Social Theory (Strathclyde University), an MMS (Sloan School at MIT), and a BA (University of Texas). He has lived all over the world, played the great game (intelligence) internationally, founded six companies and two nonprofits and lived in Manhattan for almost two decades. *www.Dr-Smith.info; www.SmithTales.com*

## Prohibition

**David Rose** writes and lectures in philosophy and although he has moved about a bit has been settled as a southerner in what he calls 'the northern wastes' of Newcastle upon Tyne, England for some time with his wife and half-Italian kids. He has published widely in philosophy, some youthful flirtations with poetry, and has published a few short horror stories, including "Onryo," in *Dark Lane Anthology Volume 5* and "Resentment Echoes" in *Horla*. *philosophervillan.wordpress.com*

## The Decay

**Sierra Simopoulos** is a Canadian writer who seeks to use her writing to make people think more deeply about ethical issues and moral tragedies that are often ignored by our society. She recently completed an English specialist at the University of Toronto which helped to develop her love of classic literature and good earl gray tea. She lives in Toronto with her wonderful husband, George.

## The Kill Registry

**Brian Howlett** is an emerging writer of fiction and nonfiction and has been published in *Exposition Review*, *Forge*, *Limestone*, *Manhattanville Review*, *Slippery Elm*, *Tulane Review*, and *The Write Launch*. He was a finalist in the Writer's Union of Canada Short Prose Competition and the ScreenCraft Cinematic Book Competition. X (Twitter): *@bdhow*

## The Crate

**David Rich** lives with his wife and two daughters in the Boston area. His short fiction has appeared in *Bards & Sages Quarterly*, *Bewildering Stories*, *Youth Imagination*, and *The Macabre Museum*. David works in the biotech industry. He holds a Bachelor's and PhD from the MIT in engineering fields.

## Form Seven Alpha

**Richard Pettigrew** is Professor of Philosophy at the University of Bristol in the UK. He started writing philosophical fiction in 2021. In his philosophical research, he asks how we should reason well about the world while being uncertain what it's like. In his fiction writing, he likes to explore questions about what we value and why, and how we should treat ourselves and others. Bluesky *@wiglet1981.bsky.social*; *www.richardpettigrew.com*

## Euthanasia

**Kelly Piner, PhD**, is a clinical psychologist who in her free time, tends to feral cats and searches for Bigfoot in nearby forests. Her writing is inspired by Rod Serling's *Twilight Zone*. Ms. Piner's short stories have appeared in *Litro Magazine, Scarlet Leaf Review, The Last Girl's Club/Wicked News, Rebellion Lit Review, The Chamber Magazine, Drunken Pen Writing, Storgy Magazine, The Literary Hatchet, Weirdbook, Written Tales* and others. Her stories have also appeared in multiple anthologies.

# Additional Information

## Reviews

If you enjoyed reading these stories, please consider doing an online review. It's only a few seconds of your time, but it is very important in continuing the series. Good reviews mean higher rankings. Higher rankings mean more sales and a greater ability to release stories.

## Print Books

*https://www.afterdinnerconversation.com*

Purchase our growing collection of print anthologies, "Best of," and themed print book collections. Available from our website, online bookstores, and by order from your local bookstore.

## Podcast Discussions/Audiobooks

*https://www.afterdinnerconversation.com/podcastlinks*

Listen to our podcast discussions and audiobooks of After Dinner Conversation short stories on Apple, Spotify, or wherever podcasts are played. Or, if you prefer, watch the podcasts on our YouTube channel or download the .mp3 file directly from our website.

## Patreon

*https://www.patreon.com/afterdinnerconversation*

Get early access to short stories and ad-free podcasts. New supporters also get a free digital copy of the anthology *After Dinner Conversation–Season One*. Support us on Patreon!

## Book Clubs/Classrooms

*https://www.afterdinnerconversation.com/book-club-downloads*

After Dinner Conversation supports book clubs! Receive free short stories for your book club to read and discuss!

## Social

Connect with us on Facebook, YouTube, Instagram, TikTok, Substack, and Twitter.

Milton Keynes UK
Ingram Content Group UK Ltd.
UKHW011917120724
445574UK00004B/341